MW01717600

sarah

a story of salvation

James R. Smerdell

Cover Illustration
Deborah A. Letterle

WORD ASSOCIATION PUBLISHERS
www.wordassociation.com
1.800.827.7903

Printed in the United States of America.

ISBN: 978-1-63385-356-0

Designed and published by
Word Association Publishers
205 Fifth Avenue
Tarentum, Pennsylvania 15084

www.wordassociation.com
1.800.827.7903

Dedication

This book is dedicated to my wife, Susanne, and my three children, Brian, Diana and Sarah. Their love and support allow anything to be possible.

Chapter 1

"Sarah."

She barely heard her name. She was in a deep sleep.

"Sarah."

This time her eyelids moved slightly.

"Sarah, wake up."

Her eyelids fluttered, she fought off the urge to wake.

"Sarah, wake up, honey."

This caused her to open her eyes and attempt to shake off the grip of the sandman. She rubbed her eyes with the back of her hands and looked around her room. There was a faint pure light in the room that was unfamiliar to her. Where was it coming from? Was she still asleep and was this a dream? She couldn't find the source of the light, but it flowed through and lit the entire room; it had no source. She sat up and allowed her eyes to focus. Looking around the room, Sarah tried to make some sense of the situation. She found the Sharper Image electronic clock on her night stand and pressed the surface button. Immediately, the digital numbers were displayed on her ceiling, it was 3:30 in the morning. Who had called out her name, was it her mom? She looked around the room again, she was alone. Sarah finally spoke.

"Who is it, who called my name? Where are you, I can't see you?"

"Don't be afraid," was the reply.

"I'm not afraid, this is my room. Why should I be afraid?"

"I believe you're not afraid," was the answer.

"I can't see you, why can't I see you?"

"I didn't want to frighten you. You are young and may have trouble understanding what is happening."

"Now I really don't understand. I can understand someone calling my name. I can understand someone visiting me in my room. What I don't understand is why you are being so evasive."

"Those are pretty big words for an eleven-year-old girl, don't you think?"

"It would depend to whom I am talking. Where are you? I can hear you, but I still can't see you."

"I'm here present with you, I'm always with you."

"How can that be? You can't be with me all the time. There are times when I want to be by myself and I close my door and stay here in my room. You can't be with me then."

"Sarah, I am with you always."

"If that's the case, then you must be God, because God is the only one that is with me all the time. I know this because I pray to him all the time and I know He hears me when I pray to him."

"You're right Sarah, I am Jesus. Why do you think I am here talking with you?"

Sarah thought for a while and asked, "Are you here to answer one of my prayers?"

"In a way, yes, I am. But can you imagine which one? You pray to me so often."

"I really can't say. I know I have been praying very hard that you help my mom find her ring. Do you know the one I'm talking about?"

"Of course, I do. It is the ring your father gave your mother before he left. Is that right?"

"You're right. You must be Jesus. Did you come to see me just because of the ring?"

"No, not just the ring. I have a gift for you and need your help."

"How can I help, Jesus? You know everything and can do everything. How can I help?"

"I always have good people help me. Sometimes, when good people help me, others listen to those good people and turn their lives around."

"So that's it, I have to help to turn someone's life around."

"You are rushing things, Sarah; I'll explain things for you."

"Should I get my mom?"

"No, you do not need her to help you understand what I want you to do."

"Why did you pick me to help you? I'm just eleven years old! I'm just a girl!"

"You are just eleven years old, but you are a good person. I need your help."

"How did you find me?"

"Your father and I have been watching over you."

"But my father is dead. I never knew my father, he died before I was born."

"Do you know how he died?"

"Yes, I do. My mom told me he died saving another man's life."

"That's right. Your father made the greatest sacrifice; he laid down his life for another. Do you understand what that means?"

"I think I do. But I really miss him. Sometimes I lie in bed at night wondering how great it would be to have a father. Other kids don't realize how much they have just by having their dad with them every day. Sometimes I cry myself to sleep wanting my dad so much."

"I know that, but I hope you understand that he has eternal life in me."

"I believe that. I learned that in religion class. Is my dad with you now?"

"Yes, he is, would you like to talk to him?"

Sarah let out a big gasp and thought about all that her mom had told her about her father.

Her father's reserve unit was activated and called into service during the Persian Gulf War. Her parents spent their last evening together at home having a quiet dinner. Before retiring, her father, Michael Martinelli gave his wife, Natalie, an eternity ring. It was customarily the tenth anniversary that an anniversary ring was given signifying the marriage would last forever. They had recently celebrated their third anniversary, they both knew they would never have another mate and they had all they wanted in each other. Natalie cried when Michael slipped the ring onto her finger. They embraced and retired to bed. It was that evening that Sarah was conceived.

Michael left for the Gulf War and never returned. His unit was following the retreating Iraqi troops as they made their way out of Kuwait. While inspecting a burned out Soviet built tank,

Iraqi soldiers opened fire on his squad and one of his men was hit in the leg. All the squad made it to cover except the wounded soldier. Michael couldn't leave him in the open and ran to his aid. He hoisted him over his shoulder and started to run for the sand dune that had been his refuge. Just before he made it to cover he was shot in the back and fell face down into the sand. His men were able to pull them to safety, but Michael's wound was too severe. His men tried to control the blood loss, but the bullet had pierced his heart and there was nothing that could be done under these field conditions. Michael looked up into the corpsman's eyes and made him promise that he would tell his wife how much he loved her. Those were the last words from his lips.

Natalie's life was destroyed. At the grave site when she was presented with the American flag that had covered her husband's casket, she held the flag close to her and cried into it. So many things ran through her mind. How would she survive without Michael? She was now pregnant. How would she be able to raise a child without her Michael at her side? How was this child to be raised without a father for guidance and love?

Somehow, Natalie did survive and did raise Sarah by herself. Natalie instilled in her Christian values and taught her how to love God and to love her fellow man. She taught her how to pray to God and to listen when he answered her. She constantly told Sarah about her father and what a great man he was and what a great father he would have been to her.

"So, you say my father is here with you," she said. "Yes, I would like to talk with him."

There was a pause, and then Michael's voice broke through the silence.

"Hello, Sarah, it's your father."

The tears swelled up in Sarah's eyes. She felt a flush flowing over her face. She didn't know how to proceed.

"It's me, Sarah, your father. I'm so proud of you. I've been watching you all your life and I can't think of any way that you could have turned out as a better person. Your mom did a great job of raising you alone. I really wish I could have been there for you. Sarah, you are so beautiful."

"Daddy," Sarah's voice was full of excitement. "I can't believe it's you. I always wondered what it would be like to really talk to you. How are you? Do you know how much I love you and miss you?"

"Believe me, I know. How is your mother, do you take care of her?"

"Yes, daddy, I love her and do take care of her. She gets sad thinking of you, especially during the holidays and your birthday. She always says how wonderful it would be to have you in our lives and how it would be to have a whole, complete family. But she helped me to understand what you did and how you gave up your life for that other man. I am so proud of you for what you did but I really miss having you in my life. But don't feel bad. Me and mom are okay."

"You are everything I thought you were. I've watched you from afar but now that I can talk to you, I know you are a remarkable girl and are very special in Jesus' eyes."

"I still don't know why you are here. You keep saying I am special, and Jesus said he has a gift for me and wanted me to help Him. Do you know what he wants? But wait, if Jesus starts talking, don't go away!"

"Don't worry, I'm here. I think Jesus would like to tell you himself why he needs your help."

"Hello again, Sarah."

"It's good to hear your voice again, Jesus."

"It is a pleasure talking with you, too, Sarah. I told you before I need your help. I want you to listen to me very carefully and if you have any questions, I will answer them. From time to time, I need to send a sign to all mankind. People don't always believe in me, but fall into a life of sin. Many people are good and follow my teachings, but others don't want to listen to my words and follow the path to salvation. I love all my creations and want them to have eternal life in me. But many want to take the easy way through life and don't want to help others but prefer to cheat and hurt one another. They don't pray to me but rather prey on each other. Do you understand?"

"Yes, I do. I watch the news with Mommy. I see how much suffering there is in the world because people are so mean to each other. Why is it that way? Why do people have to hurt each other?"

"They have free will. They can do whatever they want and sometimes don't realize the consequences of their actions."

"I see what you mean. I always have a choice to listen to my mom or disobey her. I know I could lie to her about what I do but that wouldn't be honest, and I would only be hurting my mom by not respecting her."

"That is right. Now multiply that by billions of souls that are not always honest with me and you can further understand why I am disappointed and need to do something to make people turn their lives around and seek my forgiveness."

"I understand, but how can I help you. I'm only one little girl."

"You are more than that, you are a special young lady that believes in me and has always strived to be the best you can be. That is why I chose you."

"Chose me for what?"

"I am going to give you a special gift, the gift of healing."

Sarah paused before answering; she wanted to fully grasp his words. "Who will I heal? Is it someone that is special like me? Is it someone that I know? Is it someone that is important?"

"Slow down, Sarah. You are so enthusiastic."

"Well, I always do what I'm told, particularly when it comes to you. My mom taught me all your commandments and especially the two main ones, to love God and to love my neighbor. If this is something that you want done, it must be important, and I want to know everything I can about it."

"The gift is yours to do with as you please. You will be my sign to the world that I do exist, and I do care for all of you. By simply placing your hands on someone and praying to me, they will be cured of their ailment. But they must be believers, too. That's all I ask in return. It's my sign; you will bring new hope to the world and help to change people's hearts and hopefully their lives. Men and women have to begin loving each other."

"So, all I do is walk up to someone and touch them and say a prayer to you and they are healed?"

"That's correct. You will have the power to heal through me. I will be there with you and watch over you, so don't be afraid."

"As long as this is done for you I will never be afraid," Sarah said.

"You are a brave little girl, I'm glad you will help me."

"I could never turn my back on you, Jesus. You have given me so much in my life, my mom, my health, my intelligence; you know I'm a straight A student in school?"

"I know you are. You have used your gifts wisely and with great appreciation".

Michael next spoke to Sarah. "I am so proud of you and know that you will follow Jesus' instructions and use this gift as it was intended. Do you have any questions?"

There was a period of silence and then Sarah spoke. "Jesus, do you think I could see my Daddy, just once? I know this is a lot to ask. But I've grown up without my dad for all these years and I don't know if I will ever hear from him again. Please, Oh please."

The light intensified and in the center of the room just in front of Sarah's bed, there was a swirling motion within the light. It started slowly then picked up in speed. It reminded Sarah of the cake batter in the mixer when she helped her mom bake cakes and cookies. The center of the spiral opened and there appeared the upper portion of Michael's body. He glowed like the light, but his vague details could be made out. The vision at first was blurred but came into focus. The image got sharper and sharper and then there he was. The spiral containing Michael moved up over Sarah's bed and stopped barely twelve inches from her. Michael reached out and touched Sarah on her cheek. A mild tingle passed through her facial tissue and muscles as he gently stroked her face. Sarah reached up and cupped her dad's face with both of her hands. The same tingle flowed through her hands, arms and into her very soul. Michael leaned forward and hugged Sarah. Somewhere deep inside, their souls met on some other plane of existence. Michael's and Sarah's whole bodies embraced for the first time in total completeness. They slightly released their embrace and looked into each other's eyes and smiled, then pulled back together.

"Oh daddy, I love you so much."

"I love you, too, Sarah, more than you can ever imagine."

"Daddy, can we have Mommy join us. I know this a lot to ask but just once, I want to be a whole, complete family. Please ask Jesus."

"A moment later, out of the mist surrounding them, Natalie appeared. She approached them slowly at first then rushed to hold them. The three were locked in an embrace and for the first time, they became one.

"Am I dreaming this?" Natalie asked. "This has to be a dream."

"No, Mommy, this is real. Daddy is here with us."

Michael looked into Natalie's tear-filled eyes. He reached down and softly wiped the tears from her face. He touched her cheek and bent lower and kissed her on the lips. Their lips parted, and they once again stared into each other's eyes.

"Oh Michael, you don't know how I've missed you. We were cheated of our happiness when you left me. Why did you do it, why did you have to be so brave?"

"My darling, I had to do it, it was the right thing to do. You need to understand. I would give anything to be with you and Sarah now, but it wasn't meant to be."

"I know you were right in doing what you did, but it doesn't make it any easier for Sarah and me."

The three of them continued to hold each other in silence. The swirling motion started once again and the three of them separated. Sarah found herself back in her bed watching the swirl shrink in size until it vanished.

"Don't go, Daddy, please don't leave me."

"I'm here, Sarah, don't worry."

"Daddy, I can't see you anymore. Why did you disappear from me?"

"It is time for me to go. But don't be afraid. I will always be watching over you, especially now that you are going to do Jesus' work."

"But how do I get started? Do I just walk up to someone that is hurting and heal them?"

"You will always have Jesus guiding you on your ministry, don't worry. You will know how to use your gift."

"Daddy, will I ever see you or hear from you again?"

"Sweetheart, I can't answer that. I do know that someday, you and Mommy will join me in heaven and for all eternity we will be a family. Do you understand and believe me?"

"Yes, Daddy, I do."

"That's good, honey, I knew you would. I have to say good-bye for now my brave little girl. Remember I will always be here with you, all you have to do is talk to me and I will hear you."

"Good-bye, Daddy. Remember I love you and will see you again in heaven."

"Good-bye, Sarah."

"Are you still here with me Jesus?"

"Yes, Sarah, I am."

"Will Mommy know what I'm supposed to do? How am I going to make her understand what my new job is?"

"Remember when you prayed to me and asked that I help you find your Mommy's ring?"

"Sure, I do. It was the ring my dad gave to my mom before he left us. It is my mom's most precious gift. She was so sad when she lost it and still tells me how much she hopes she finds it."

"Tell your mom to look in her jewelry box where she usually kept the ring when she wasn't wearing it. It will be there as a sign to her. It will help her to understand and believe."

"Thank you, Jesus, for finding her ring, I know she will be happy and understand what you want me to do." Sarah paused and wondered how she should address her next question to Jesus.

"Sarah, what is wrong. I sense you want to ask me something but are hesitating to do so."

"Jesus, do I have my gift now?"

"Yes, you do."

"And can I use it however I want?"

"That is what I told you."

"Jesus, may I use my gift and heal my father and bring him back to Mommy and me?"

"Sarah, I'm sorry, but that cannot happen."

"Why? I don't want to question you but why can't I, if the gift is mine to use as I wish?"

"Your father is with me in heaven. Everyone's time on earth is just a test. A test to see if you believe in me and follow my laws. If you listen to my words and obey my commandments, you obtain your ultimate reward, which is heaven. Your father has obtained his reward of eternal life. He is in my presence. His spirit needs nothing more. He would never want to return to his earthly body."

"Not even to be with me and Mommy?"

"Not even to be with you and your mother. He is at peace."

"I understand Jesus, he has you and doesn't need anything else."

"Sarah, I am leaving now. Remember that I will always be with you and you do not have to be afraid. People will see you and believe. You will help to save their souls."

"Thank you, Jesus, for letting me and my mom see my dad. I think Mom will have some peace now. I promise to do what I'm told and never let you down. I will use my gift as you told me, I promise."

"You are good, Sarah Martinelli. I know I have made the right decision in choosing you. I will be with you always. Good-bye, Sarah."

And with those closing words, the pure light in Sarah's room faded away into darkness.

Sarah was still sitting up in her bed. She let herself lie down and pondered all that had happened. She reached over and touched her clock and the time displayed on her ceiling. Once again, it read 3:30. Was this all a dream or had she really seen her dad and talked with Jesus. She knew this was real and that she had a mission to perform. What about the time on the clock? How had she had the discussion and visit with Jesus and her dad, yet no time had passed? She couldn't comprehend these things, but they didn't bother her. After all, what was time to Jesus? Sarah rolled over and, in a few moments, fell into a deep sleep.

Sarah awoke again to the sound of her name. This time, her mom was sitting on the edge of her bed. Natalie bent over and stroked her hair back from her face and kissed her.

"Wake up honey. It's Saturday and we have a lot to do today."

Sarah, coming out of the sleep state thought to herself, if you only knew, Mom, if you only knew.

She reached up and put her arms around her mom's neck and pulled her face down to hers. She kissed her mom and said, "Good morning, Mom, I love you."

"Well, I love you, too, sweetheart. How did you sleep?"

"Like a rock, Mom. How about you?"

"I had a really strange but lovely dream last night."

"Mom, it was no dream, it really happened."

"What are you talking about dear; you didn't let me tell you what my dream was about. And besides, it was a dream so how can you say it was real?"

"Wasn't I in the dream with you?"

"Why, yes, you were."

"Didn't it feel real to you?"

"Yes, it did. But how do you know what I dreamed about?"

"Because it was real, and I was there with you and dad."

Natalie looked down into Sarah's eyes and searched for some sense to this conversation. How could Sarah know what she dreamed about? How could Sarah know the dream was about Michael? How could Sarah know the three of them were together?

"Darling, how do you know what I dreamed about? Was I talking out loud in my sleep? Did I wake you up and did you come into my room and listen to what I was saying to your dad?"

"No, Mom, it really happened. Dad was here last night and visited with us. He was here with Jesus!"

"Oh honey, there must be some other explanation. I must have talked in my sleep and you overheard what I was dreaming about."

"No Mom, Dad was here, and he appeared to me and he let me invite you, too. It was a wonderful visit. We hugged, and you got to talk to Dad. He told you he did what he did because it was the right thing to do. He told you how much he loved us and not to be afraid."

Natalie studied her daughter's face and tried to put it all together. She was a rational person, always looking for the facts and never letting her emotions run wild. But how could Sarah know about her dream in such detail? It was as though she really was there in her dream sharing that space with Michael.

"Mommy, I have a sign from Jesus to show you that what happened was real."

"Now dear, don't let your imagination run wild. This is just a coincidence. You must have overheard me in my sleep."

"I can prove that it all happened. Come follow me."

Reluctantly, Natalie was led by the hand down the second-floor hallway to her bedroom. When they got to her bureau, Sarah said, "Okay, Mom, now open your jewelry box."

"What do you mean?"

"As a sign, your anniversary ring is back in your jewelry box."

Natalie first looked into Sarah's wide eyes then over to the box sitting on the top of the bureau. With trembling hands, she held the side of the box with her left hand and slowly opened the lid with her right. As the box was about halfway open, Natalie gasped. There, in the front fold of velvet was her ring. She fully opened the box and slowly reached for the ring. She picked it up and slid it onto her left ring finger. She walked backward until her legs touched her bed and she sat down. Natalie felt very light-headed as she sat, staring down at her hand. How could this have happened? How did the ring suddenly reappear in the jewelry box? She had searched for it for the last month since she lost it. She thought that she would never see it again. It meant the world to her. It was the last gift that she had received from Michael.

She reached out and lifted Sarah onto her lap. With tear-filled eyes, she pulled Sarah to her chest and hugged so hard, Sarah thought she would pass out.

"Sarah," Natalie said, "I need you to tell me what is going on here. How did you know the ring was going to be in my jewelry box? How did you know about my dream? I need you to tell me the truth."

"Mommy, I always tell you the truth."

"I know you do, darling, but I don't understand what has happened here."

"Jesus said he would help you to understand by this sign. Do you understand?"

"Sweetheart, I understand that the ring is back in my jewelry box, but I don't understand how it got there."

"Jesus put it there, so you would understand and believe."

"Understand and believe what? I believe in Jesus. I believe he is good and looks after us since your daddy is gone. What else am I to understand?"

"Jesus has given me a special gift."

"What kind of a gift? Is it something I can see? That will help me to understand and believe."

"No, you can't touch his gift. He gave me the gift to heal the faithful."

Natalie studied her daughter's features, looking for some way to comprehend what was transpiring. But she found no relief and continued to question Sarah.

"Tell me everything that happened, don't leave anything out."

"First Jesus came to my room and he woke me up. He said he was very happy with me and wanted me to help him. He wanted to give me a special gift that would prove He exists. He said it would help people to turn their lives around. Then Daddy appeared in my room. He hugged me, and I asked if you could join us. He said yes and then you appeared. We all were together for the first time."

"I remember that, but I thought it was all a dream."

"No, Mommy, it really happened that way. I asked Jesus if I could use my special gift to heal daddy and have him come back to us, but He said that wasn't possible. Daddy is happy with Jesus in heaven."

"What does he want you to do with your special gift? That part I don't understand."

"I have the power to heal people as long as they believe in Jesus. I am to use this healing gift as a sign to all men and women that Jesus is real and cares for us. He wants all of us to pass the test here on earth, so we can be happy with him in heaven for all eternity just like Daddy."

Natalie couldn't believe what she was hearing. Sarah did point out that her ring was returned to its place in her jewelry box and she did know about the details of her dream. Was it possible that she was chosen by Jesus to help turn around the lives of men and women? How could an eleven-year-old girl possess such power and use it properly? Why did Jesus choose her Sarah? For the next hour Natalie and Sarah sat on her bed and Sarah told her everything that had happened in full detail. Natalie searched for some answers and suddenly her heart was filled with the Spirit. A calming yet exhilarating wave spread through her consciousness and she believed and understood. It would be her responsibility to protect Sarah and help her complete her ministry.

Natalie wanted to be sure to follow her mandate and sought out the advice of her pastor. She called and scheduled an appointment with her parish priest. Fr. Mark Wilson was an elderly priest nearing retirement. He loved to spend time each day in his garden that was located on the west side of his rectory building. His parish was located on the rolling hills of their suburban community. During these pleasant spring days, he prepared his garden for the upcoming season. Each day he followed his regimen of weeding and hoeing and planting and watering. His garden was always the envy of all his neighbors. The garden was Fr. Mark's only passion in life and because of this he endured the pain of advanced arthritis.

Natalie arrived on time for the appointment. Fr. Mark had just come in from his garden and was covered with top soil and he was sweating profusely through his clothes. Fr. Mark scrubbed his hands in the sink in his mud room and wiped the sweat from his face and forehead with his hand towel. Natalie shook his hand and gave him a little hug which was their custom.

"Fr. Mark, I must seek your counsel. Something wonderful has happened to Sarah that I must share with you. She has received a gift of such importance and magnitude that I have to be sure it is used properly and without perversion."

"Perhaps you should start at the beginning, Natalie".

Natalie spent the next twenty minutes relaying the story to Fr. Mark. She tried to include all the details, so he would fully understand the challenges that lay ahead. When she was finished, she searched Fr. Mark's face for some sign that would indicate whether he believed or was skeptical of her story. Fr. Mark finally spoke.

"Natalie, I don't know what to say. I have heard of faith healers before although I have never put much credence in their abilities. Has Sarah made any attempts to use her gift?"

"No, Father, I wanted to seek your counsel first. Do you believe me? Do you believe that something this wonderful could happen to my Sarah?"

"I've been around for so many years in my ministry and hardly anything can surprise me anymore. But this is certainly unusual. Can I meet with Sarah and talk with her? I think once I talk with her I'll know better how to proceed."

"Of course, Father. Why don't you follow me home? Sarah is staying at my neighbor's home while I'm here. Sarah loves you and will speak freely with you."

Father Mark agreed but insisted he be allowed to take a quick shower and change before meeting with Sarah.

Fr. Mark drove his car and followed close behind Natalie. When they arrived at her home, Fr. Mark was let inside while she went to her neighbor's home to collect Sarah. When Sarah entered her home and found Fr. Mark sitting on the living room sofa, she ran to him and dove into his arms.

"Hi, Fr. Mark, it is so nice to see you. How's your garden coming along this year?"

"Just fine, Sarah, just fine. And how are you doing? I understand something wonderful has happened to you and I'm here to talk with you and help to sort everything out."

"I think I know what happened to me and I know about the special gift I have received. I think Mommy just wants to be cautious that I follow Jesus' instructions carefully and do all that he wants me to do."

"Do you believe Jesus came to you and bestowed on you a special gift of healing?"

"Oh yes, Fr. Mark, I do."

"Sarah, what you are saying is very serious. You shouldn't make these statements lightly. You don't want to make Jesus mad at you."

"Why would he be mad at me? He came to me. He asked me to help him. He told me I have to help people save their souls."

Fr. Mark sat back on the sofa. His many years were clearly starting to take their toll on him. He let out a sigh as he studied Sarah's face.

"Sarah, before we let the public know of your gift, we have to be 100 percent certain that you have received this gift, these special powers. We can't be careless."

"But Fr. Mark, Jesus told me to do this. If He told me, how can it be wrong?"

"No, no, no, my child, I didn't say you were wrong or not telling me the truth. You must understand that there are always people out there that want to harm others and steal from them. They lie and cheat others for their own gain."

"I know this, that's what Jesus told me. How can I prove to you that what I am saying is true, that what happened really did happen to me?"

"As I said before, we must be certain that you have this special gift before you can start your mission."

"Fr. Mark, why don't you let me touch you and pray for you and when you are healed, that will prove I am telling you the truth."

"My dear, how can you heal me?"

"But Fr. Mark, I see you moving slowly all the time and especially when you work in your garden. You have rheumatoid arthritis and it causes you great pain. Your fingers are twisted, and you have a lot of trouble holding your chalice at Mass. Let me help you."

"Sarah, I'm an old man. I've spent my whole life following my vocation to be a priest and doing God's work. It's not right that I be cured. Why would you want to waste your gift on this old man?"

"If I can prove it to you then nobody can deny that Jesus is real and wants to help people."

Before he could say another word, Sarah reached out to Fr. Mark. She placed her hands on his shoulders and closed her eyes. Her lips started to move as she prayed to Jesus and requested that He help Fr. Mark and heal his ailments. Fr. Mark lowered his head and began to recite the Our Father. A feeling of great warmth flowed from Sarah's touch into Fr. Mark's body. He could feel the healing powers rush through his tissue, muscles, bones and organs. The warmth was so comforting that he wished it would never stop. A flood of emotions sprang up within him that could not be defined by mere words. Fr. Mark was witnessing a miracle, his own miracle. His body responded by straightening up on the sofa. He found renewed strength that he hadn't experienced for so many years. After a short period, Sarah released her grip on his shoulders and sat back on his lap.

Fr. Mark opened his eyes and started to cry. He attempted to speak but wasn't sure the sounds he was making were real words that could be understood or just mumbled gibberish. He wiped the tears from his face and once more attempted to speak. The phlegm in his mouth was thick and he had to wipe his mouth before attempting to speak.

"My Lord and my God" were the first words out of his mouth. "It's true, Sarah, you have been blessed."

Fr. Mark had Sarah slide off his lap and stood up for the first time in many years without pain. He stretched to the left and then to the right. Like an athlete in a gymnasium ready to begin an exercise regimen, Fr. Mark bent over and touched the tips of his shoes with his fingertips. He let out such a deep belly laugh that he startled Sarah. He looked down into the face of his healer and tears welled up again.

"Sarah, you are special, you have been given a remarkable gift from Jesus and my faith in God has been renewed. You are one of God's little angels."

Fr. Mark reached down and picked up Sarah. He held her in his arms and didn't want to let her go. He knew he was in the presence of one of God's chosen ones. He just stood there, holding Sarah. Then a sense of fear and dread came over him. How could he protect Sarah? Natalie coming to him must be a sign that he had to be involved in this little one's life, that he must help to protect her and her gift. He must safeguard the gift and prevent its exploitation. But how? He finally collected his thoughts and spoke to them.

"Natalie, Sarah, I believe you and will do all I can to protect you from those evils in the world that would pervert this gift into something that it was not intended to be. We must go to my Bishop and seek his advice."

"Fr. Mark, I know you love me and want to protect me, but I don't think that is what Jesus wants me to do. He said he would be by my side and would protect me. He said the gift was mine to use as I wanted, and that people would see this sign and believe. Why do we need more help? You know that I'm telling you the truth. You know that I can heal with my special gift. What else is there to do? I'm ready to start using my gift to help people."

"Sarah, sometimes it takes the clear thinking and unprejudiced eyes of a child like you to set even an old man like me straight. You're right. If Jesus is on your side, how can anyone hurt you?"

Fr. Mark stayed with Sarah and Natalie for dinner then left for his rectory in the early evening with a renewed sense of faith. He vowed he would pray for Sarah's safety and that the hearts of men and women would be opened to God's love and forgiveness.

Sarah was curious how she would first use her gift. Although she had healed Fr. Mark, she considered that just a test of her God-given powers. She wanted to charge out into the world with limitless energy and spirit to help everyone that she could. Sarah knew that if she placed her trust in Jesus, He would reveal to her how and when to use her gift for the first time. Her first encounter didn't take long to present itself.

Chapter 2

Monday morning, Sarah stepped from her school bus and was walking toward the entrance of her elementary school building. It was a beautiful spring morning and she felt the warmth of the sun bathe across her face. She felt good about herself and held the secret of her special gift close to her heart. She was about to enter the building when she heard a most horrific sound. The father of a student was in a hurry to drop off his child and get to work. He had a busy day scheduled and needed to get to work to finish a presentation that was due in the afternoon. He didn't notice the crossing guard in front of him and at the last minute, to avoid hitting her, swerved his SUV and hit a parked school bus in the rear right corner. The impact was severe enough to flip his vehicle over on its side. The fuel line ruptured and within seconds, a fire start under the hood and spread by the leaking gasoline onto the road surface.

All the adults in the immediate area ran to the scene. The SUV was on its side which made the evacuation of the occupants very difficult. The driver from Sarah's bus placed the vehicle in park and set the parking brake. He unhooked the fire extinguisher over his seat and rushed to the accident. The fire was brought under control in a matter of seconds, but the passengers were still trapped. The driver of the SUV was unconscious and resting on top of his daughter, pinning her to the door.

Sarah's bus driver used the base of the extinguisher to smash the windshield until it looked like multiple spider webs. He then peeled away the broken glass and finally had access to the victims. After the father's seatbelt was snapped open, he was removed from the cabin. His daughter was in tears, not moving, but grasping the handle of the door. The bus driver finally reached in and pulled her to safety. The little girl was in considerable pain. The impact of her father's body against hers when the SUV flipped had broker her forearm and caused a compound fracture. The razor-sharp edges of the radius and ulna bones in her left arm were protruding through the muscles and tissues and blood was flowing profusely from the wound. The little girl was going into shock from the pain and loss of blood. The bus driver ran her over to a grassy area and gently laid her down on the soft green surface. He quickly applied pressure to the wound, as an attempt to stop the bleeding. He screamed at the top of his lungs for assistance.

Sarah had been watching all these events from her vantage point on the top step of her school. But something very peculiar was happening. All the events happened in slow motion. To her, it was a surreal experience. She saw the SUV come to a stop after it flipped, but it seemed to take forever to come to rest. She saw the flames start to spread around the vehicle, but they seemed to lap at the hood like a child enjoying an ice cream cone; each lick was a slow, methodic flicker of the tongue of the flame. She saw her bus driver moving from her bus and running to the SUV with the fire extinguisher in his hand. But it reminded her of an old news clip she had seen of an astronaut running across the surface of the moon; every step was a prolonged leap that caused the muscles in his body to ripple as his foot hit the surface of the street. She knew this was a sign to her; she had to get involved with this situation.

She started to walk down the steps and headed toward the area where the little girl was placed. As she moved closer, the speed of the scene around her quickened until she was moving in synch with her surroundings. There was a small crowd gathered around the little victim, but this did not deter her. Sarah bravely moved through them until she was hovering over the little girl. She stared down at her and immediately recognized her. It was Victoria McMurry, a second grader she knew from her neighborhood. Victoria was not moving, and Sarah noticed that the color of her complexion wasn't normal. Victoria looked very pale. Sarah knelt at her side and tried to console her, but Victoria was not responding to her kind words. Sarah started to reach for Victoria's left arm, but the bus driver brushed her arm away and told her to move back and that this was no place for a little girl.

Sarah, not discouraged by his comments, again reached for Victoria's arm and this time succeeded in gently grasping it in her hands. The bus driver wanted to push her away as he did before, but something stopped him. He felt as if he was paralyzed and totally out of control of his body. He watched as Sarah gently held Victoria's arm and closed her eyes. He heard her mumble something, but he couldn't make out the words. Sarah just knelt there, eyes closed, as if in a trance. He was so intent on watching Sarah that it wasn't until a few seconds later that he heard the others that had gathered around the scene start to gasp in astonishment. He looked down at Victoria's left arm and saw the arm straighten out, the bones disappear beneath the skin and the bleeding stop. A few seconds later, Victoria's color returned to her cheeks and she opened her eyes. Sarah opened her eyes and gently placed Victoria's arm at her side. A large smile appeared on Victoria's face as she looked up at Sarah.

"Hi Sarah. What is everyone doing standing around me? Where's my daddy?"

"You are okay now. You were hurt but you are safe now."

"What happened? I remember my dad drove me to school and I remember pulling up to the front of school."

"There has been an accident and you and your dad were hurt. You're okay so let's get you over to your dad so we can check on him."

Sarah stood up and with Victoria at her side, moved through the crowd. The bystanders parted without objection as the two little girls moved through their midst. Most spectators had expressions of disbelief on their faces, unwilling to accept what their senses had perceived.

Victoria's dad was still unconscious and lying on the grass not far from where Victoria had been placed. They approached her father who was covered by a blanket that one of the bystanders had pulled from their trunk and placed over him. Victoria immediately ran and fell to the ground next to him. A few seconds later Sarah arrived and knelt next to her.

"Daddy, wake up, wake up daddy," Victoria cried out. She was scared at seeing her father lying helplessly before her. "Sarah, what is wrong with my daddy, why isn't he waking up?"

"I don't know, Victoria, but there is no reason to be afraid."

With that statement still echoing in her head, Victoria witnessed the strangest thing. Sarah leaned over and placed her hand on Mr. McMurry's forehead. She closed her eyes and started to say something. Victoria, not able to hear, said to Sarah, "What are you doing to my dad, what are you saying to him?"

Sarah seemed not to hear her and kept her stance. A few moments later, Mr. McMurry could be heard clearing his throat and started to open his eyes. Looking up and seeing Victoria's face, he raised his arms to her as he had done so many times before and pulled her to himself. They both hugged so hard it could have hurt.

“Victoria, thank God you’re okay. I remember our car going into a roll, but I can’t remember anything after that. How did we get out? How did you escape injury?”

“Daddy, it was Sarah, she saved us.”

“Wait a minute, Victoria,” said Sarah, “I didn’t pull you from your car, I only helped to heal your arm.”

“What’s this about her arm,” asked Mr. McMurry.

“Victoria’s arm was broken from the crash and I was able to pray for her and she was healed,” said Sarah.

“Now dear, you must be mistaken. I’m sure her arm was hurt, I can understand that. But you couldn’t have healed her. Let me see your arm.”

Victoria raised her left arm and allowed her father to examine it.

“No dear, let me see your other arm, the one that was hurt.”

“But daddy, I did hurt my left arm and Sarah healed me,” Victoria insisted.

“I’m sure that’s what you believe but let me get up and I’ll get to the bottom of this.”

By this time, the paramedics had arrived and rushed over to them. The first to reach them was Chuck Roberts. He approached them and asked where the accident victims were. He had been dispatched to aid an unconscious adult and a small girl with a compound fracture of the left arm. Sarah was the first to speak.

“Everything is okay now. I think the only thing that needs help is the car, it’s still on its side over there.”

“That’s not funny little girl, I need to know where the injured people are. We can’t afford to waste any time,” said Roberts.

"I'm not being funny, and I am serious. Everybody that was hurt is okay now. I said a prayer and healed them both."

"Okay, I've had enough of this."

Roberts stood up and started to walk around the immediate area looking for the victims. He finally approached a small group of bystanders and asked where the accident victims had been placed. One individual pointed to the location where Victoria had been lying. They then told Roberts what had happened and insisted that they had witnessed a miracle.

Sarah decided she could do no more to help. She walked the short distance to her school building, entered, and made her way to her home room and her seat. A warmth filled her to the core. She knew she was doing Jesus' work and helping those in need. What better calling then to serve our Lord and others?

As other students arrived, they joined in the busy talk about what they had heard and seen outside. Ultimately, they pointed in the direction of Sarah, comparing their stories and wondering about the extent of her powers. When their home room teacher, Mrs. Dorothy Hemmerle entered the room, she was amazed at the activity and volume of noise emanating from the group. Her usually sedate students were buzzing like bees and the sound was deafening. She finally got them under control and into their seats. Not having been present for the activities outside the school building, she was unaware of the events that had transpired. She walked over to Sarah's desk and got down on one knee to be at Sarah's eye level.

"What's wrong, Sarah," she asked. "What's all of this hub-bub?"

"Nothing, really, I just helped people in need outside the building and I guess everyone is curious about what I did," she said in reply.

"What did you do that has everyone buzzing?"

"Mrs. Hemmerle, it's a long story and I don't want to take up class time. Can we talk at recess or maybe at lunch time?"

"Sure, honey, let's get our busy day started. We have numerous tests scheduled for today and a review on two more subjects. Please see me at the recess break."

With that, Mrs. Hemmerle got up off her knee and went to the head of the class. She got the class focused and had her students recite the Pledge of Allegiance. Next, she informed them of the scheduled test in math and handed out the test forms. Sarah's classmates were quiet during the math test but the buzzing among them started again after the test. Mrs. Hemmerle had to quiet them down repeatedly throughout the day.

At recess, Sarah approached Mrs. Hemmerle's desk as the other students left the room.

"Hi, Mrs. Hemmerle," Sarah said sheepishly, "would you like to talk now?"

"Sure, let's go to the crafts table in the corner and sit there."

They both walked to the back of the classroom and took seats at the table. Mrs. Hemmerle was very curious about the events of the morning. Her usually well-behaved class had to be quieted many times and this disruptive behavior could not be tolerated.

She started by asking Sarah, "So, would you like to tell me what happened this morning that has your classmates all worked up?"

"Mrs. Hemmerle, I'm sorry that the class kept talking today. I guess it's only natural for everyone to be surprised when they witness a miracle."

"What do you mean a miracle?"

"I mean a real miracle. Do you know Victoria McMurry in the second grade?"

"Yes, I do, I taught her older brother."

"You were probably in the classroom this morning when she and her dad were involved in an accident outside. I'll tell you what happened. Her dad hit a parked school bus with his SUV and it flipped over. A fire started but my school bus driver put it out quickly. When Mr. McMurry and Victoria were pulled out of their car, they were both seriously injured. Victoria had a broken arm and Mr. McMurry was unconscious. I went over to each of them and was able to heal them both. I know this sounds kind of crazy, but I've been given a special gift from God to heal."

Mrs. Hemmerle sat there in silence for a time, going over Sarah's words in her mind. She wasn't quite sure how to proceed. She wanted to be supportive of Sarah, but she also didn't want to encourage her in what initially sounded like a fantasy. She finally spoke.

"Okay, you told me what happened this morning but how did you arrive at having this special power?"

"It's not exactly a power because it doesn't come from me; it's a gift from Jesus. He came to me two nights ago and asked me to help him. People are hurting each other, and a lot have lost hope. By giving me this special gift of healing, He made me his messenger. It's my job to help people see that there is hope in our loving God and obeying his commandments."

"Have you used this special gift before this morning?"

"Oh yes, me and my mom met with Fr. Mark yesterday and I cured him of his arthritis."

Mrs. Hemmerle knew Fr. Mark. She was also a member of his parish. She decided she would place a call to Fr. Mark after she was done talking with Sarah.

She looked down into Sarah's eyes and sensed an inner peace that she hadn't seen in someone so young of age. Sarah's life was difficult at times because she was raised by her mom and truly missed having her father in her life. Sarah's mom was a great mother. Mrs. Hemmerle and she had been friends in school and occasionally attended social functions together. Was Sarah's story factual or was she allowing her creativeness to get out of hand? It was not her intention to press Sarah any further or make her feel uncomfortable. She was going to call Sarah's mom and perhaps Fr. Mark as well. She would get to the bottom of this. She didn't want the disruption that happened in today's class to continue and she wanted to make sure Sarah wasn't having any emotional problems.

"All right, Sarah, that will be all. Let's join your classmates."

"Mrs. Hemmerle, it seems like you don't believe me. I'm telling you the truth. Everything I've told you actually happened."

"I'm sure you believe what you told me is true, it's just that I will do some further checking. And we can't allow the disruption to continue in our classroom. We're here to learn and you know there is little time for foolishness."

"Thank you, Mrs. Hemmerle, for listening. I never wanted to cause any problems for you."

With that, Sarah got up from the table and left the room. Mrs. Hemmerle sat there and pondered what Sarah had told her. Sarah was a bright girl and Dorothy Hemmerle didn't want her to suffer because of her overly creative imagination. She would call Fr. Mark immediately.

Fr. Mark answered the phone as he usually did, half out of breath.

"Hello, this is Fr. Mark," he said, "how may I help you."

"Hi Fr. Mark, it's Dorothy, Dorothy Hemmerle."

"Oh, hi Dorothy, to what do I owe this call. Aren't you at school?"

"Yes, I am, Father. But I need to ask you a few questions and I think it's important enough to call you now. My class is on recess, so I don't have a lot of time," she said. "Something strange has happened at school today and I need your input. Sarah Martinelli was in class today, but that's not the issue. My students were restless all morning and the reason appears to revolve around Sarah. She claims to have witnessed an automobile accident this morning. Two people were hurt in the accident and Sarah claims to have healed them. When I talked to her about the experience, she said she visited with you and healed you. Can you shed any light on this? I'm worried that her imagination may be running a little wild and I don't want the class to suffer any further disruptions."

There was a silence at the other end of the line for so long that Dorothy had to ask if Fr. Mark was still on the call.

"Yes, I'm still here and yes, Sarah did visit with me and yes, she did heal my arthritis. I was wondering how long it was going to take for this to get out. All she has told you is true; she was touched by God and given a special gift. It is now her mission in life to bear witness to the Lord and spread the good news of hope and love. She is to act as God's messenger and help to turn the lives around of those whom she helps. I talked to her mom and wanted to seek the guidance of our Bishop, but Natalie insisted it wasn't necessary. God has set the path for Sarah and no one can stop what is set in motion. All we can do is pray for our little Sarah and trust in the Lord."

Fr. Mark's emphatic tone surprised Dorothy. He was generally a very meek man, but the strength behind his voice made her shudder. If Fr. Mark could get this excited about what appeared to have happened to Sarah, how will everyone else deal with this life-changing event?

This time it was Dorothy who remained silent and it was Fr. Mark who had to roust her from a thoughtful trance. "Dorothy, Dorothy, are you there, do you understand what I just said?"

"Yes Fr. Mark, I heard you, but I don't know what to make of it."

"There is nothing we can do but pray for her, believe me, this is out of our hands."

"I agree. I must go now; my children will be coming back from recess. Good-bye Fr. Mark."

"Good-bye, Dorothy."

And with that, they both ended the call.

The activity outside of the school seemed to ebb and flow all day. Local news crews arrived to cover the accident but soon got caught up in the frenzy of chatter surrounding the rumored miracles that had occurred earlier that morning. Each crew took their turn interviewing bus drivers, EMS personnel, pedestrian witnesses and crossing guards. Images and statements of the reporters and their witnesses soon jammed the airwaves of the local TV and radio stations. More and more vehicles arrived on site to cover the media event that eventually the school parking lot and surrounding streets were a gridlock full of satellite transmission vans and marked station SUVs. It was only a matter of time before the local police were alerted to the turmoil and responded with multiple field units.

Students, teachers and school administrators watched the show from the safety of their classrooms. The school principal remained steadfast in refusing access to the building and Sarah by the media. But the school day would soon be at an end and the students would have to leave on their buses. It would take some serious site management to clear the area for the buses to enter and exit the school grounds. It was apparent to the police sergeant in charge on the scene that the situation was out of control and becoming a safety issue. He began to push back the news crews from around the building and made sure the adjacent streets were kept clear. Late in the afternoon, the buses arrived to ferry their precious cargo home.

Dorothy Hemmerle continued to monitor the activity on the school grounds all day and knew that once Sarah left the safety of the school, the media would be relentless in their pursuit. She arranged for a police escort for Sarah's bus but knew that might not be enough. She placed a call to Sarah's mom to forewarn her of the impending danger. Natalie thanked her for her thoughtfulness and devised a plan of her own. She told Dorothy to get word to Sarah that she must exit her bus two stops before her regular stop and she would be waiting there for her.

Natalie watched all day as a cadre of news anchors and curious onlookers continued to assemble in her neighborhood. She repeatedly refused to answer her door, finally posting a sign that simply said, "GO AWAY!"

Fifteen minutes before Sarah's usual drop off time, Natalie slipped out her back door and made her way through the back yards of her neighbors. She finally arrived at the intended bus stop that she had instructed Sarah to use. As soon as the bus came to a halt, Natalie arrived at the exit doors just as they were opening. Sensing the urgency of the situation, her classmates had Sarah ready at the door as it opened so she could make a speedy exit and escape. The two backtracked the way Natalie had come and soon were safely inside their home. They made their way to the second-floor front bedroom window to watch the circus unfold. As Sarah's school bus arrived at their street corner, its doors opened. Two children stepped from the bus and immediately were accosted with a barrage of questions, "Are you Sarah Martinelli? How long have you had your powers? How did you get them? Do something for us now!"

Natalie was happy they had avoided the encounter with the media but knew this was just the beginning of a lifetime of stress and worry. She searched her heart and wondered how others she knew from the Bible had coped with the notoriety: the prophets who were rejected and banished by their own people, the early Christians who were persecuted for their faith. But she realized she couldn't crawl into a hole or bury her head in the sand forever. How was that doing God's will? Almost as soon as she had that thought, a sense of relief came over her, like a sweet breeze of spring flowing over her face. She knew in an instant that God was helping to quell her fears and guide her through these first few days. She looked at Sarah just as Sarah looked at her and somehow, they both felt the same release of tension. They reached for each other and felt that beautiful breeze surround and envelop them. After a while, they walked down to the first floor and opened their front door to face the crowd.

Natalie settled the crowd down and stated that she would agree to have three news crews come into her home in thirty minutes. She would allow them to choose among themselves which three would be the lucky ones. With that, she closed the door. Immediately, the bickering started among the crews. It continued for some time until one rational reporter persuaded all the crews to agree to pull straws. It sounded rather primitive, but no one else could come up with a better way. It was decided that the three longest straws drawn would determine the fortunate crews that would gain admittance to the Martinelli home.

The only room in the humble little home that could accommodate the crowd that would soon assault their sanctuary was the living room. Natalie hurriedly moved lamps and end tables and placed kitchen chairs and folding chairs in every available spot. The room looked so cramped and cluttered that when she finished she felt embarrassed at allowing anyone in, but these were unusual times.

She swung open the front door and found an orderly crowd assembled. The fortunate crews that would soon be granted admittance had done their homework. They researched what they could find about the family and knew that Natalie's husband, Michael Martinelli, had been killed saving another soldier during the Gulf War. They also knew that Natalie and Sarah were the only two living at this address. Out of respect for this family that had made the ultimate sacrifice, the crews acted professionally and entered the home in an orderly fashion. Natalie guided them to the living room where they all took their seats. The news reporters took the front seats while the camera crews and producers filled in toward the back. Natalie apologized for the cramped conditions but felt it important that she and Sarah meet with the local media now instead of allowing the furor to continue. She introduced Sarah and began her statement. The cameras began to whirl, and the high intensity camera lights switched on and beamed directly at her. Natalie was temporarily blinded but soon her eyes became adjusted and she spoke.

"First of all, thank you for agreeing to my demands and acting in such a professional manner. The last three days have been very difficult for the both of us, but it is just about what we had expected." Natalie was visibly shaken and had to pause and collect herself. One of the reporters in the front row, seeing her apparent discomfort, reached up and gently touched her hand. She gave Natalie a reassuring look which seemed to calm her a little. Natalie continued. "My husband died, and Sarah has been raised in a household with only one parent, me. I'm naturally overly protective of her; she is only eleven years old. I'm sure that if you're a parent, you realize that your child is your greatest treasure in life. You will do anything to protect the child no matter the circumstances or even how old the child becomes. So, it is with Sarah. Until Saturday, I protected her and gave her the best life I could. But on Saturday, our world changed, your world changed.

"I don't know how much you know about the happenings at Sarah's school today. Early in the morning, there was an accident and two people were seriously injured." Natalie looked at the faces staring back at her. Their eyes were so intently focused on her, she felt as though she were a hypnotist, casting a spell over them. "Sarah witnessed the accident and got directly involved."

The reporter that had touched Natalie's hand marshaled enough courage and interrupted her by questioning, "What do you mean, she got directly involved?"

This was the moment they were waiting for; they all froze in their seats. Natalie thought for a minute then contemplated the time she had spent with Sarah early Saturday morning, when she first became aware of Sarah's gift. She committed herself to her daughter's mission and would never hesitate in its fulfillment or second guess its nature. With these thoughts, her spirit was strengthened.

"Through God's loving mercy, Sarah healed them."

There was such a gasp that you would have thought the air was totally sucked from the room. Through their many interviews, they had heard the same story over and over all day. They didn't expect Natalie to be so straight forward with them and reinforce what they had heard earlier in the day. The front row reporters turned in their seats to face the rolling cameras and each began to editorialize the encounter. Seeing the outburst,

Natalie knew she had to bring this interview back under her control. She didn't want a three-ring circus in her home. Sarah's mission was something special, something sacred and not to be trivialized. She had to repeat herself before the reporters ended their observations and turned in their seats to face Natalie.

She said, "I will ask you to allow me to finish my statement and then I'll answer any of your questions. Please don't do that again. This is hard enough." The reporters and crews sheepishly sat in their seats like children who had been scolded; they got the point.

"Sarah had a visit, no, call it a revelation, on Saturday morning. She was given a special gift, the gift of healing. We met with our priest, Fr. Mark Wilson, to find some sense, some rational meaning to all that had happened. What you don't know is that Fr. Mark and not the two members of the McMurry family was the first to feel God's healing graces. Fr. Mark met with us and naturally, had his reservations about the validity of our story. Sarah followed Jesus' instructions and prayed over Fr. Mark and almost instantly, his arthritis was cured. If you know Fr. Mark Wilson, you know he has been plagued with this ailment for many years. He used to struggle just to finish Mass each day. But now, his pain and discomfort have been removed from his life and he is a believer in the mission that has been given to Sarah. He suggested we approach our Bishop prior to the start of Sarah's mission but we felt it unnecessary since we were following God's will. You are aware of the happenings at Sarah's school this morning so now you know everything there is to know. I will answer any of your questions, but please keep them relevant to this matter. For Sarah's sake, I will not entertain any inquiries into our private lives."

Almost instantly the hands went up. The types of questions arose that you would expect from a skeptical group. After a while,

Natalie saw the interview was deteriorating. She felt compelled to prove once and for all that Sarah's gift was authentic.

Don Stokes was one of the reporters seated in the front row. He was a local icon among news reporters. In his seventies, he was without a doubt one of the oldest reporters still active in the nation. Starting in the business with the advent of the television, three generations had grown up seeing him on the news and had come to trust in his reporting. Natalie and Sarah were among his faithful followers. She knew that if Sarah could touch and heal Stokes of his ailments, it would go a long way in convincing the unbelievers that what Sarah had was real and holy and not to be considered a circus side show.

Natalie asked Stokes to please rise and approach her and Sarah. Natalie said, "Don, I don't want to put you on the spot, but we need a so-called guinea pig to lend credibility to my statements. Would you be willing to assist me?"

Stokes rose and stood next to Natalie with a somewhat puzzled look on his face. The unusual contortions of his face were accented by his rather large glasses. Throughout all the years of working long hours in his profession, reading page after page of copy, typing on old mechanical typewriters through the age of the word processor, he had paid the price of deteriorating eye sight. The frames of his glasses were oversized just to handle the Coke bottle bottom lenses he needed to see. Additionally, he had a small hearing aid inserted in each ear. He wasn't quite sure if it was his love of rock-n-roll music or his working in all the different venues over all these years that had caused his near loss of hearing. But here he was, standing next to this mother that professed her daughter to be a faith-filled healer. Why was he selected and where was this going? He soon found out.

Natalie looked at Sarah and without a word, Sarah approached Stokes. She looked up at him and asked if he would please lower himself to his knees, so she could hold him and pray over him. Without question, Stokes got down on his knees in front of Sarah. It wasn't easy for him, considering his age, but he complied. Sarah reached out and removed his glasses and handed them to her mother. She next requested that he remove his hearing aids and after he removed them and switched them off, Sarah gave them to Natalie. Sarah instructed Stokes to close his eyes, which he did. With everyone in the room staring intently, Sarah reached out and cupped Stokes' balding head in her hands. She began to pray in a low tone that was barely audible. The cameras were rolling, and the high intensity lights were still centered on this spectacle.

Stokes felt something happening to him. A sense of warmth and comfort emanated from his very core. He wasn't sure of its source but eventually knew it was coming from Sarah's touch. He thought to himself, how can this be? Is this a hoax or is it real? All the years of searching for the truth and approaching everything from a rational standpoint defied this moment. He only knew he didn't want the strange, comforting feeling to stop. He came back to some semblance of reality when he heard Sarah say, "Amen." She released her hold and took a step back. She then told Stokes to open his eyes.

"I'm afraid," were the only words he could utter.

"Don't be afraid, you have been given a gift," said Sarah.

Stokes opened his eyes slowly. It took a minute to focus because of the strong lights, but eventually he was able to open his eyes completely and looked around. The first thing he saw was Sarah's smiling, angelic face just a foot away from his. He reached out and pulled her close to himself. He whispered something in her ear that was only meant for her to hear. She whispered something back to him. His eyes began to swell over with tears of happiness. He had truly witnessed a miracle and it had been his own. He was a believer. Not only was he able to clearly see without the aid of his oversized glasses but for the first time in many years, he heard the sounds that surrounded him without the aid of a mechanical device. The sounds were pure and were lacking the metallic qualities to which he had become accustomed. He stood up and turned to face the cameras. A broad smile came across his face as he spoke.

"It's true, she has a special gift, and I have been healed. I'm not a man who gives into unsubstantiated facts. I've been trained over many years to search for the truth, and when you uncover the truth, no matter how unsettling it may be, the truth is the truth. Sarah's gift is real. I don't know any other way of saying it. Through these circumstances, I've been given something special. Why was I the one chosen to be here today? Why was I the one chosen to receive this gift? It could have been any other reporter, but I was the one picked. I can't ignore what has happened to me, it was for a reason. I'm glad I was picked. Maybe my reputation for honesty and thoroughness came to bear, I don't know. But you all have witnessed this miracle and now must report it faithfully as you have seen it."

That wasn't going to be a problem. Each camera used in the room was connected by cables back to their news truck outside. Each truck had a satellite transmitter mounted on its roof and the entire encounter was beamed into space and returned by satellite back to earth and received at the three local news stations. Once the interview with Natalie started, none of the news stations wanted to lose the opportunity of being the first to break the unusual story so they interrupted their normal broadcast with this news item. They weren't sorry they did. The minute Stokes had finished his statement, the entire interview was sent to each station's parent location. That night, the story would hit the national news and shortly thereafter, the world would know.

Stokes turned to face Natalie and Sarah. He stepped forward and reached for Natalie's hand. Instead of offering her hand, she put her arms around him. After a few moments had passed, they separated. Natalie turned and retrieved his glasses and hearing aids from the end table on which they were placed and handed them to him. He looked down at them and once again, his eyes swelled with tears. He looked at Natalie and said, "when I came to your home to cover this story, my heart was hardened. I was ready to grill you and your daughter over this and expose you as frauds and cheats, trying to gain fame and notoriety. Now, I must apologize for my ignorance and ask for your forgiveness. I had no way of knowing that Sarah's gift was authentic, and she was truly touched by God. I promise you I will do all in my power as a Christian and as a reporter to spread the word of Sarah's mission and I will bear witness that her gift is bona fide."

The crews started to tear down their equipment when Sarah suddenly approached them. She said, "I have to tell you that while I was praying over Mr. Stokes, I was also praying for you." With that said, she walked over and touched each individual. The same warmth and curing feeling experienced by Stokes also entered each of them. One of the production crew had the early stages of macular degeneration which was instantly reversed. Another's hypertension and elevated level of cholesterol was brought under control. She moved from person to person and each knew of their health conditions and how they had been cured by this young woman of God.

Sarah finally came to Debbie Mitchell, a young reporter getting her reporter's teeth cut on her first big story. Sarah held out her hand for Debbie to grasp and instantly became aware of the impending danger lurking inside of her body. Sarah looked up into her wide eyes and said, "Debbie, you are truly fortunate to have come here this evening. I know that you are having a baby, but I must tell you that a horrible cancer was spreading throughout your body and would have killed you and your baby. The outward signs of the pregnancy masked the symptoms and by the time the cancer was diagnosed it would have been too late. You are cured, enjoy your baby."

Debbie became so light-headed over the news she started to pass out but was caught by her coworkers and placed back into her seat. Each person in turn gratefully acknowledged the gift they had received and profoundly thanked Sarah. Debbie Mitchell quickly recovered and joined in with the accolades placed at Sarah's feet.

Sarah came to Stokes' side and he looked down into her soft eyes. He went down on one knee and hugged her. He told her not to be afraid of her gift and that people will come to her in sincerity, seeking her help. He thanked her for her courage and wished her God's continued protection. He finally had the courage to ask, "Did you cure my baldness? Can you get me a mirror?"

Sarah paused for a moment then said, "Don't press your luck."

With that, everyone in the room let out an enormous laugh. It was more of a relaxation of emotions after all that they had experienced.

It was getting late so Natalie asked if they could wrap things up. One of the reporters asked, "What will you do now?"

"That's a very good question," Natalie said. "I'm sure this will unfold as God has planned it."

The news crews finished packing their gear and were escorted to the front door by Natalie and Sarah. Each person thanked them and promised they would complete their editorials and follow-up reports with total honesty and fairness to them.

Don Stokes lingered with his farewell noticeably longer than the others. He just didn't want to leave this blessed family.

Outside of the Martinelli home, a crowd too numerous to count had gathered. The saturation on every TV, cable and radio channel of this unbelievable story had caused the number of spectators to swell into the adjacent streets and alleyways. But somehow all remained calm, they just wanted to hear from the fortunate few who had first-hand access to this remarkable family. Stokes took the lead and recounted to the crowd who were within hearing distance the events of the last hour. He became emotionally overwhelmed as he described the interview, the healing process, and subsequent farewells. The crowd hung on his every word. To summarize, he asked that they respect the family's privacy and disburse. Nothing more would be happening tonight and there was nothing to be gained by keeping vigil outside of their home. Somehow, the masses understood and were moved with love and concern for the little angel inside the house. Each in their own way said a silent prayer for Sarah and took their leave of the area.

While lying in bed that evening waiting for the grasp of sleep to overcome her, Sarah pondered the events of the day. She had finished her prayers and had rolled over and found her little nest for the night. Visions of the morning activities outside of school were recalled. She thought about the discussion she'd had with her teacher, Mrs. Hemmerle, and finally the news interview late in the afternoon. Not bad for the first day, she thought. But then she started to question what was to follow. Where is Jesus leading me? Am I doing what I'm supposed to be doing? I'm only a little girl, how am I supposed to know what to do. With these doubts lingering in her mind, she finally felt mentally exhausted and gave in to her body's demand for sleep.

As she sank deeper and deeper into the abyss of sleep, she suddenly felt her entire being floating above her surroundings.

Complete darkness soon encompassed her. For a moment she became frightened but then in an instant, she entered a realm of pure light. This time, the bright light had a source and she focused on it. As she stared into the light, she felt herself being drawn into the light. She offered no resistance. She had to know the reason for this journey. Was it a dream or was Jesus calling to her?

Sarah entered the light and found herself on some level of existence outside of reality and the physical world. She felt as though she were standing on something solid. When she lowered her eyes to see, she noticed there was nothing there to support her, only the pure light which seemed to go on forever in all directions. She became frightened and cried out, "Where am I, what am I doing here? Jesus, have you sent for me?"

She heard a comforting voice and with that voice a gentle calming ensued. "I am here with you, Sarah."

The voice was a familiar one, she had heard it one time before. "Jesus, it's so good to hear your voice again. Where are you, I can't see you."

"I can take any form, but I know how you perceive me to be. Don't be frightened, I will now appear before you."

Off in the distance, Sarah caught the slight movement of a shape that disrupted the even flow of the pure light. She had no idea how far away the figure was because from her standpoint it was impossible to judge any distance in her current surroundings. The blurred figure continued to change its shape as it moved closer to Sarah. The vision at first appeared to Sarah like a kaleidoscope, its parts swirling with many colors and variations of light. Eventually, the swirling motion stopped, the colors stabilized, and the form of a man appeared from the chaos. Standing before Sarah, Jesus smiled down on her and she returned the same.

Jesus took on the soft features of a statue that Sarah prayed to each time she attended Mass. He wore the traditional white tunic and red robe we have come to expect along with open-toed sandals. His hair was shoulder length and he had a full beard.

"May I hug you?" were the first words she could utter.

"Certainly, my child."

Sarah leaped forward into his outstretched arms and felt his soothing graces flow into her soul. After a while, she noticed He felt warm to her, a comforting warmth. But was there really a variation of temperature in this spiritual space? With her face buried in his robes, she perceived a beautiful scent, like the smell you get when you first walk into a floral shop, that pure, clean, bouquet of scents from so many different flowers in bloom. But were these scents real or imagined? As she hugged Jesus, she continued to roll these thoughts over and over in her mind.

Jesus said, "Be calm, I feel your uneasiness. As I said before, I appeared to you as you perceive me to be. I know of your love for flowers and how you linger in the floral shop when you and your mom go there. I want you to remember this experience, using all your senses in the process. Do you understand?"

"Yes, I do. But, where am I? Is this heaven?"

"No, this is not heaven. It is a place that exists neither on earth nor in heaven." Sarah released her hold and she and Jesus joined hands and began to walk through the light, somehow supported in this spiritual place.

Jesus continued, "I brought you here to meet with you and to tell you how proud I am of you. You did an excellent job today, handling yourself in difficult surroundings. You remained calm and fulfilled my instructions to the letter. But that was just the first day. Now that word of your special gift has been unleashed on the world, things are about to change."

Sarah nodded in acknowledgment of what He was saying. They continued to walk together, hand in hand.

"You know, Sarah, I could have chosen anyone to help me with this task. Do you know why I chose you?"

"You told me that I was faithful to your commandments, I prayed often, and listened to my mother. Is that why?"

"That and more, He said. You are an innocent child without prejudices or ill will in your heart. People will see you for what you are and understand that you have no ulterior motives or self-serving intentions. I could have chosen anyone, but you have been unwavering in your love and faithfulness."

"Have you asked many others in the past to help you and if you have, have you appeared to them and helped them the same way you are helping me?"

"I have asked many in the past to assist me with my work. Most of the time, I touch their hearts and they are moved to do extraordinary things. When they do and remain faithful to my calling, we call them saints. Sometimes, following my wishes, they make the ultimate sacrifice, we call them martyrs."

"My dad made the ultimate sacrifice, didn't he? Is he a martyr?"

"No, he is not a martyr. The brave act your father did was out of compassion for a fellow soldier. He shares everlasting life in me for what he did out of free will. Everyone has free will, sometimes it's used for the betterment of others, and sometimes it's used to prey on others. Many make bad decisions and fall out of grace with me. They misuse their free will."

Sarah listened intently as Jesus continued.

"I created each of you out of love and expect you to love God and one another as you love yourself. This rarely happens. Instead of focusing on the important things like worshiping God and caring for family, spouses, and tending to those who are in need and suffering, people want to amass great wealth and power. There is nothing wrong with either except when they are used improperly, by enslaving others through control and neglect. This must stop. People need to care for one another and focus on the things that will obtain them eternal life. Each person comes into this world with nothing and that is how they leave. What you obtain in life doesn't matter, how you use it does. And it's not only material wealth, but knowledge and time that must be shared. Parents must provide their children not only with the material necessities but also their love and time. Today's society has evolved such that the pursuit of wealth overshadows the love and nurturing of its children. Little time is left at the end of the day for parents to hold their children and look into their eyes and tell them how much they are loved. Parents who have aged are no longer cared for by families but warehoused in senior homes and forgotten. Worshiping God is no longer a priority but severely neglected. Faith must be shared and passed on. You are one generation away from the unfaithful."

Sarah understood what Jesus said. She felt a change taking place deep within her that made this possible; Sarah was maturing. She still had the appearance of a blond haired, blue eyed eleven-year-old girl but mentally and spiritually, she was growing beyond her years. Sarah felt this change and embraced it knowing it was due to Jesus' will. This maturity would be required for her to administer her first gift. There would be many challenges for which she must be prepared. It was the second of many gifts that Sarah would receive over time, each received as it was needed.

As they walked, Sarah listened to every word spoken by Jesus. She thought of how it must have been for Jesus' disciples, the apostles, to walk with Jesus and hear his sacred words. And now, it was she in his presence, listening and preparing for her ministry just as the apostles prepared for theirs. She didn't want this time with Jesus to end but knew it wouldn't last much longer.

They stopped walking and Jesus turned and faced Sarah. He reached down and cupped His hands around her face and tilted her head upward. He looked deep into her eyes and asked her, "Do you understand what just happened to you and how you are to use your second gift?"

Sarah said, "I can't put into words the change that just occurred, but I know how it is to be used. This second gift is the gift of wisdom. It will allow me to deal with individuals on every level. I will have the ability to converse with believers as well as non-believers. It will help me to use my first gift in many different circumstances with patience and humility but always for your praise and glory. Thank you."

Jesus said, "I know you will succeed."

He continued, "Your mother will need to know how she is to support you in your ministry. I will touch her heart and she will understand her part."

Jesus released his hold then reached out and pulled her close and hugged her one last time. She felt the same glowing warmth as earlier and marveled at all they had discussed.

She asked Jesus if they would meet again and He assured her they would. He reminded her that He would always be with her and would protect her from adversity. They parted from the embrace and each said a good-bye.

The pure light started to dim and with its passing so did the vision of Jesus fade. Sarah knew she would soon be back safe and sound in her bed and the night would pass away as usual.

Still in a conscious state and waiting for sleep to overtake her, she contemplated the effects that the second gift would play on her mission. She felt she understood her mission more completely but at the same time was presented with new challenges. Now that she viewed things from a mature perspective, a myriad of challenges presented themselves to her. How would she deal with the overwhelming crowds? How would she handle the unbelievers who would question her legitimacy? What would happen when an unbeliever wasn't cured, would there be retaliation on her or her mother? The anxiety continued to build to a crazy crescendo.

She had experienced anxiety in the past. Certainly, in anticipation of a final test at school or waiting for a holiday or special occasion came to mind. She had always been able to control these issues, but the newly perceived problems were overwhelming to her. But suddenly, she became aware of something special that night and she immediately attributed it to her newest gift. A profound peace came over Sarah-the fullness of peace that can only come from God. She understood now that by putting her faith and trust totally in God freed her spirit of unnecessary stress and worry. By freeing her mind and soul of things not under her control she would be able to completely and without reservation attend to her duties. She could now find happiness and relief knowing that she was fulfilling her mission. It was the gift of wisdom that allowed her to find this peace. A gentle smile came across her lips as she slipped back into a much-needed sleep.

Chapter 3

That evening, like so many others in the metropolitan area, Bishop Daniel Wallace watched the news. He had heard earlier in the day of the alleged miracle that had taken place and was anxiously waiting to see the news media tear this family apart and prove them to be frauds. From the comfort of his study, he watched the news teams that had assembled in that woman's house. They were listening to her lies and the Bishop listened intently as questions were posed to her. She seemed pretty much in control and unflappable. The thing that particularly caught the Bishop's attention and made his blood pressure rise was the remarks made by this woman about one of his priests. Apparently, Fr. Wilson was aware of this self-proclaimed healer and did nothing to stop her. He was even a party to this charade. How could one of his priests not inform him of this travesty unfolding in his diocese let alone participate in this hoax? So, Fr. Wilson was healed, the Bishop thought. No one was going to get over on him. How that charlatan could be allowed to run freely in his diocese without paying the consequences. That little girl must be stopped. The Bishop was so wrapped up in his ego that he failed to watch the remainder of the footage and see the true miracles unfold on the screen. He called to his aide and demanded that he track down Fr. Wilson and have him come to his quarters immediately. He could have handled this over the phone, but he wanted to see Fr. Wilson squirm in his presence. This was an evil trait to the Bishop's character. He found great pleasure in his control over people and used every opportunity to exercise his power over his subordinates.

Fr. Wilson received the call and a devastating chill ran up his spine. He knew in his heart that he should have talked with his Bishop concerning Sarah, but after their meeting and dinner together he took Natalie's advice and placed his trust in the Lord. This apparently was about to backfire.

Fr. Wilson hurriedly finished his supper and raced to the Bishop's house where he was escorted into the study. There he found the Bishop behind his huge hand-carved wooden desk with a look on his face that would have certainly halted any army in its tracks.

The Bishop started with, "Good evening, Fr. Wilson. I see you have been involved with this little self-proclaimed healer; there can be no denying it. I heard the mother state that you were aware of this girl's claims and participated in the hoax. What do you have to say?"

Fr. Wilson was in utter disbelief. He was standing upright before his Bishop and the Bishop didn't notice how erect he was. So many years had passed with Fr. Wilson crippled over from his arthritis, his hands barely able to hold his chalice during mass. His need for a cane later in life was his means of maintaining his mobility. But now this pompous *servant of God* stood there chastising him for his actions when the truth was staring him in the face the whole time.

Again, the Bishop challenged him, "What do you have to say for yourself?"

Fr. Wilson did everything in his power to contain his anger. After all, this was his superior and he must address him with respect for his station regardless of his feelings.

“It is true, on Saturday I met with Mrs. Martinelli and her daughter Sarah. They are a family in my parish. I’ve known them for many years. I’ve baptized Sarah, regularly hear her confessions and gave her First Communion. Her mother, Natalie, is also a practicing Catholic in good standing with the church.” He paused then continued.

“Something extraordinary has happened to Sarah, something wonderful. Our Lord and Savior has chosen her to be his special emissary; she has been given the wonderful gift of healing. She is to use this gift to make people everywhere aware of Our Lord’s presence in the hope of turning their lives around. This is a mission from God that cannot be denied. I’ve been witness to it, just look at me. I’m standing here before you upright for the first time in years. My pain is gone, my mangled hands are straight and true, I feel like a young man once again. How can you deny what you see in front of you?”

For the first time, Bishop Wallace stopped to take the time to look at the man standing before him. During his inquisition and the follow-up statement by Fr. Wilson, the Bishop never really stopped to look at the man. His position afforded him this power over people and he rarely looked at anyone while addressing them. He now sat in utter amazement at the revitalized man standing before him. Occasionally, over the years, Bishop Wallace felt a sense of pity for the plight of the crippled Fr. Wilson but never inquired as to how he was feeling or if his assignment at his parish was too much for him to handle. But now, there he was, standing tall and pain free, and proclaiming that that small girl was the instrument of God that perform his miracle.

Bishop Wallace mulled over in his mind all that had transpired. How might he take advantage of this situation to heighten his position in the church? If this girl truly had this healing gift and she resided in his diocese, he should receive the notoriety and fanfare. Much of the attention should be channeled in his direction, after all, he was the Bishop.

He thought for a short time longer then said to Fr. Wilson, "I must meet with this girl immediately. I feel it is my responsibility to care for her and protect her and make sure she is following God's will to the letter. I need you to take me to her."

Fr. Wilson saw clearly through the Bishop's plot and wanted to put a halt to it but wasn't sure how he could. He had taken a vow of obedience and never failed to honor that commitment. Now his Bishop wanted to exploit this little girl's gift for his own glory and furtherance of his career and he felt helpless to stop him.

"But Bishop Wallace, it is late. The family has been through quite an ordeal today and I believe their privacy should be respected. With the story of Sarah's gift hitting the airwaves tonight, they are going to be overwhelmed with people wanting access to her powers and I don't know how they will be able to survive the onslaught. Allow me to call Mrs. Martinelli tomorrow and arrange for your meeting."

"No, that is unacceptable. I will not have access to her if the crowds get to her tomorrow. I need to meet with her in a dignified and controlled manner. You must call that woman now and set up the meeting for this evening."

Fr. Wilson was close to exploding at the Bishop. He was trying to be reasonable, but the Bishop had his own agenda and Fr. Wilson knew from experience that you don't disagree with the Bishop once his mind is set. He finally acquiesced and reached for the phone. Fr. Wilson got Natalie's number from directory assistance and placed the call.

Natalie's house phone was ringing nonstop since the news interview. The local phone lines were starting to be affected by the call volume and soon something would have to be done.

Natalie looked at the caller ID on her phone and refused to answer any call with an unfamiliar number. She saw the ID of the latest call originating from the Bishop and considered answering the call. Remembering her conversation with Fr. Mark she was hesitant to pick up the handset but against her better judgment she did. Fr. Wilson could tell from the tone of her voice that it had been a rough and trying day for the family. Fr. Wilson finally spoke.

"Hello Natalie, it's Fr. Mark. I saw the interview you permitted today for the news media and have to say you and Sarah handled yourselves quite well. It had to be very difficult but as we had talked, this was to be expected. It was the first of many steps to be taken to announce to the world of Sarah's God-given powers and to set her ministry in motion. I think you both are very brave, and you are continually in my prayers. How are you?"

Bishop Wallace listened intently and wished that Fr. Wilson would cut the small talk and get to the point of the call.

Natalie took a deep breath before speaking. "Fr. Mark, it is great to hear your voice. To answer your question, it was a tough day for us. But with the help and prayers of so many, we made it through the day. I notice you are calling from the Bishop's phone. What's up?"

"Bishop Wallace summoned me after seeing the news interview from earlier today. He has concerns and since we reside in his diocese he wants to meet with you."

Fr. Wilson weighed his words carefully since the Bishop was hanging on every word he spoke. Fr. Wilson felt he was betraying the trust he had established with Natalie, but he felt he was boxed into a corner and had no choice. There was a pause on the line and neither of them spoke for an uncomfortable time.

Bishop Wallace's patience ran out and he grabbed the handset from Fr. Wilson.

"Hello Mrs. Martinelli, this is Bishop Wallace. I hope we aren't catching you at a bad time."

Fr. Wilson thought to himself, what is this man saying? Certainly, this is a bad time. Look what this family went through today. But the consideration of others was never the Bishop's strong suit. The Bishop continued.

"I was fortunate enough to see the interview you and Sarah gave today and am totally amazed at the maturity and grace in which Sarah handled herself. You must be very proud of her."

"Yes, I am. I have always been proud of my daughter. She has had a difficult life growing up without a father, but she turned out very well. She turned out well enough to please God so that's all that really matters."

Bishop Wallace had not done his homework or any other research and didn't know anything about how Michael Martinelli lost his life and how Sarah had been raised in a single parent home. His prejudices just assumed the father had abandoned the family.

"I agree we must all do everything in our power to follow God's will and his commandments." There was another pause while the Bishop prepared his words carefully. "I'm compelled to meet with you and Sarah to validate your claim. You reside in the diocese in which I am Bishop, so it is my responsibility to ensure this is not a mockery of our faith and truly something originating from God. I believe we should meet immediately."

"That is impossible. I have already put Sarah to bed. She had a trying day and tomorrow promises to be even more difficult for her. We are doing the best we can and so far, Sarah has followed her instructions and initiated her ministry with unwavering faithfulness."

The Bishop didn't like to have his requests refused. When he spoke, he always got his way. He had to respond and get control back in his corner.

"I see. Well, how about meeting first thing tomorrow morning, say about 7:00 AM? I can have my driver bring me to your home then."

"Bishop Wallace, I really don't think a meeting is necessary. Sarah has received a very special gift from God. She has been instructed on how she is to use her gift and so far, she has followed her instructions to the letter. I think God is pleased with her, so any validation of her mission isn't necessary."

This disregard for the Bishop's request greatly disturbed him. Fr. Wilson could see the stress building within him. He was waiting for the next shoe to drop.

"Mrs. Martinelli, I can't have you and your daughter running around in my diocese proclaiming to be faith healers and on a mission from God without the direct oversight of my office. This just can't be allowed. I will not permit it."

"Bishop Wallace, Sarah's mission did not originate from any church on earth but directly from God. I really don't think that the church must validate that which originates from God. God does not have to answer to anyone."

"Mrs. Martinelli, you are treading on very shaky ground with your statements. I must insist on meeting with you and your daughter."

Natalie knew this conversation wasn't going anywhere and gave in to his demands.

"Seven tomorrow morning will be fine."

"A broad smile came over the Bishop's face; he had gotten his way by exerting pressure and the treats of possible retaliation.

"Very good, Mrs. Martinelli, I will see you then. Good night."

"Good night to you, Bishop."

They both hung up their handsets.

Fr. Wilson was appalled at the events that had transpired before him, but he realized he was powerless to alter the situation. He asked the Bishop if it was necessary to accompany him in the morning, but the Bishop said Fr. Wilson had done enough damage and wouldn't be needed at the meeting. Fr. Wilson wished the Bishop well and took his leave. On Fr. Marks's drive home his thoughts were on Natalie and Sarah and he intently prayed for their safety. He also prayed for the Bishop and hoped his hardened heart would be softened.

Natalie finally retired after the Bishop's call. So many issues ran through her mind as she was attempting to get some rest. Will she and Sarah be safe from the expected mobs tomorrow? Will her home be safe, and their limited privacy respected, or will they be inundated by visitors and phone calls? How will this ministry affect Sarah and her life? Will she lead a somewhat normal life and grow to be a beautiful woman as Natalie had always hoped or will her gift weigh down on her so much that she loses her life too early? What about the Bishop's visit tomorrow, how will that go? Natalie's world was swirling out of control with all these issues. She needed some relief of the pressure and stress of being a concerned mother. It would soon come.

As sleep overcame her exhausted body, she became aware of a presence in her subconscious. It was as though she shared her mind with another entity. Was she losing her mind? She thought. Were all the events of the last few days taking their toll on her mental stability? Natalie opened her mind to all possibilities and finally realized she was in contact with the spirit of God. Sarah had seen the emotional drain occurring within her mother. She could see the stress and apprehension in her face and in her voice. Sarah loved her mother unfailingly and needed assurance from Jesus that her mom would completely understand her mission in support of Sarah and not be afraid of their safety. It was because of Sarah's concerns that God's spirit was embracing and comforting Natalie. Natalie's complete being was elevated to some unimaginable level of serenity; spiritually, physically and mentally. She touched the face of God and found a mixture of emotions that quelled her restless soul. There was a profound happiness that she had never experienced before, not even at her wedding or the birth of her child. There was a calmness that could never be equaled, not even compared to one of her most memorable days that she and Michael had spent resting on a blanket under a tree in the springtime, staring up at the cloud filled sky and marveling at the beauty that surrounded them. There was a sense of a boundless love that went beyond the love that can be comprehended by any mortal, it was agape, the unconditional love. Natalie wrapped herself around this sense or feeling of God and God totally encompassed her. She saw an unending vision of the kindness and love of God, and for the first time in her life understood the true meaning of love and the giving of one's self without restraint. These emotions, these feelings, she couldn't determine how best to describe the experiences, permeated every fiber of her being. She found the faith she needed to believe in Sarah's mission without doubt. She found the love she needed to understand the upcoming needs of the people Sarah would meet and seek her healing touch. And lastly, she found the hope she needed to trust in the Lord that Sarah would be safe and successful in the administration of her gifts. Natalie embraced these gifts of the Spirit and found complete internal peace. She knew all would go according to

God's plans and that putting her faith and trust in God was the only way to have any understanding and comfort in Sarah's undertakings. All the stress and concerns were lifted from her and she fell into a deep and restful sleep.

Tuesday morning came like any other, but the world had changed overnight. As the news footage was shown over and over in virtually every market around the world, people everywhere were renewed in their faith and found new hope in the Lord. Many would hurry to their place of worship and pray to the Lord with such sincerity and intensity as never before. Many accessed computer systems to find the exact location of Sarah and started to formulate plans to make a pilgrimage to witness her miracles firsthand. Yet others disavowed the truth presented before their eyes and hardened their hearts. This seemed to create a greater division between the faithful and the faithless than ever before.

Natalie and Sarah awoke to the bright rays of sun piercing through the slats of the blinds that protected their rooms from the outside world. Sarah slid out of her bed, slipped on her robe and slippers and ran down the second-floor hallway to her mother's room. She found her mom sitting up in bed but there was something different in her appearance, so much so that she stopped in her tracks. Natalie looked up and their eyes met. Instantly, Sarah could see the change that had come over her mom and she knew the source. She ran to her mom and dove onto the bed. They embraced and that same peace and comfort that Natalie had experienced last night was shared by both.

Sarah looked into her mom's eyes and said, "Now you know what it is like to see God. Now you know what it is like to experience his peace and love. It says in the gospel writings that Jesus would approach his disciples after his resurrection and address them with 'Peace be with you.' It wasn't until they received the Spirit that they understood what he meant. We are so fortunate that we have experienced the peace and love of God and are to be instruments of his great works."

"Oh Sarah, I didn't fully understand everything until last night when I received the Spirit of the Lord. I had my reservations and fears and wondered why this enormous burden was placed on you. Why would a young girl have to be an instrument of God and carry out his work? Why not choose an adult who could rationalize it all and have a better grasp on the tasks at hand? But last night my heart and mind were opened to the Spirit and it all became so very clear to me. I now know that you will be safe, and people will be positively affected by your actions. I am here to support you in your mission and help clear the way for people of every faith to approach you and find that which is lacking in their lives. God was wise in choosing you. I know the content of your heart and character and will follow you to the ends of the earth."

"I asked Jesus that He touch your heart and give you peace and He answered my prayer. I am so happy you are comfortable with my God-given gifts and more importantly that you now have found tranquility in your life. I know it has been tough not having Dad to be in and share our lives. You had to be a mother and father to me. I believe I will never be able to express how much I love you and respect you for all that you have given to me and done for me. You have given me a life filled with love. You have nurtured me in mind and in spirit. You have made sure I wanted for nothing. You have been both model and hero to me. For all that you have done for me I can only simply say, thank you."

They embraced. Natalie knew that in many ways she had lost her daughter. The innocent little girl in her arms was no longer her little girl. In a matter of a few days Sarah had matured to the level needed to effectively minister to the faithful. A sudden sadness encompassed her thoughts which were immediately felt by Sarah. Sarah released the tight embrace and grasped Natalie by the shoulders. "Mom, I will always be your little girl, don't worry. God has been kind to us and has given us so much. Have you wondered why we succeeded so well without Dad? God was watching over us and made sure we had everything we needed. You always had the right kind of jobs that gave you the flexibility in caring for me before and after school. We always had friends in our lives that were there when we needed help. Remember the time that the furnace broke in the middle of winter and how the repairman came to our house on a Sunday night to fix it? He knew we were two helpless females and showed compassion for us. How about that old car that we relied upon that always needed repaired? The salesman who gave us a new car below his cost was in the same reserve unit as Dad and went out of his way to take care of us. These were all acts of kindness but guided by divine intervention. We must now give back for all that we have received. And it is with great joy that I can fulfill these tasks with you at my side, my mom!"

Natalie marveled at the insight and level of maturity that Sarah now possessed. She felt confident that with the oversight of the Lord, she and Sarah would be safe from harm and be able to effectively and wholeheartedly complete the tasks now at hand.

Sarah said, "Now, let's get ready for the Bishop."

"How did you know about the Bishop coming this morning? I talked with him last night after you went to bed."

"It was revealed to me, and I know just how to handle this situation."

Natalie sat in amazement with her mouth agape as Sarah rolled off the bed and skipped down the hallway. A servant of the Lord but still my little girl, she thought as a broad grin spread across her face. All will be well.

AS per their agreement, at 7:00 AM sharp, the Bishop's limousine arrived and worked its way through the crowd that had remained on vigil outside the Martinelli home overnight. The Bishop exited the vehicle after anxiously waiting for his driver to open his door and offer a hand to assist him. He was a rather rotund man who always gave in to his desires. Food and drink were a great joy for the man of the cloth and he never passed up an opportunity to indulge in these passions. The years had taken their toll on his waistline, but it never seemed to matter to him; his appearance was never challenged or critiqued.

He had the power to do as he pleased, and many priests were disciplined for objecting to his policies and banished to rural, out-of-the-way parishes where they could do no further harm. Bishop Wallace had one objective in his crosshairs and that was his elevation to be the next cardinal in the United States. He quelled every dissent in his diocese and made sure every scandal was swept under the rug. He positioned himself to always grab the limelight when participating in the national Bishops' conference and always made the headlines during his frequent trips to Rome and the Vatican.

But today his world would drastically change. He had greatly underestimated the eleven-year-old girl waiting for him behind the door at the top of the steps. He truly believed this would be a slam dunk for his career in the church and assure him of his appointment as the next cardinal. But God had other plans for him. He would now have to account for the many years of abuse to his priests and the faithful for which he was responsible. He had been placed in a very powerful position and had misused that power for his own gain and amusement. It was time to pay the piper.

Bishop Wallace grasped the handrail and started up the steps leading to the front porch and door. He immediately broke into a sweat even though the morning was cool, and the sun had not made its direct appearance on the property. He stopped at the door to regain his breath and composure before knocking the first time. All of ten seconds passed and there was no answer of the door. This time he made a fist and banged heavily on the door. How dare they keep me waiting, he thought.

Natalie and Sarah had just finished a light breakfast and placed the dishes in the dishwasher when the first knock was heard. They looked at each other and a smile gradually formed on their lips. A twinkle had now shown in Sarah's eyes that made Natalie smile that much more. Through her revelation, Sarah had come to know that she was about the Lord's business in preparing for her ministry and this was a necessary step in the process. The Bishop had all the intentions of using and manipulating Sarah down a path that would have jeopardized the intent of her mission. For self-gain, the Bishop wanted control of Sarah and to control how the gifts were used. This may have been his plan, but it certainly wasn't God's plan. He would now have to pay the price for his arrogance.

The door was slowly opened, and Natalie and Sarah were revealed to the outside world. Film crews that had patiently waited all night had their cameras rolling and reporters were giving insight to the current happenings. The reporters could barely be heard over the roar of cheers and chanting that emanated from the untold number of bystanders hoping to get a look at the latest celebrities to hit the airwaves. Many were there out of pure curiosity but many more of the faithful were there hoping to be blessed by this angel of God. They understood in their hearts the meaning of these incredible events and were caught up in the true spirit of the time.

Natalie opened the door wider and stepped out onto the porch. She had to ask the Bishop to please step aside so she could address the gathered crowd. The Bishop grudgingly obliged and made a mental note to later refer to the assembled faithful as a mob and that Sarah would surely need his guidance and protection.

As Natalie approached the top of the steps, an instant hush came over the crowd. They looked up with hope in their eyes and wanted to bear witness to this amazing event. After what seemed an eternity, Natalie turned and signaled for Sarah to join her. Sarah walked out of the house passed the Bishop and stood next to Natalie. People started to cry and were overwhelmed at the sight. People raised their hands, begging Sarah to come down to them and minister to their needs. Bishop Wallace was not used to being brushed aside in this manner and was ready to approach the two now standing in front of him when the little girl did something amazing. After looking up to her mother as if to get an approval, she walked down the steps and proceeded into the middle of the crowd. With fearless strength and a presence about her, Sarah greeted and prayed over the assembly. Sarah closed her eyes and stood in their midst praying to the Lord for his healing graces. She opened her eyes and started walking, all the while touching the hands and foreheads of all that she could reach. One after the other, people of faith experienced a healing of spirit, mind and body and realized a renewed sense of love and hope in the Lord.

Everyone reacted to their gift in a different manner. Some simply closed their eyes and marveled at the experience and their recovery from their ailment or disease. Others broke down in tears and collapsed to the ground thanking and praising God for his kindness. Still others experienced nothing at all. These were the unbelievers that were there to ridicule Sarah and participate in what they believed to be a circus atmosphere. After a while they, like many more to follow, would become believers and turn their lives around.

The cameras continued to run and capture the incredible event from every possible angle. Bishop Wallace saw this as the opportunity of a lifetime and started down the steps to intercept Sarah. Natalie tried to stop him, but she was no match for his considerable girth. As he hit the pavement, he started through the crowd. Amazingly, people parted the way for him respecting his position in the church. It was like Moses parting the Red Sea. When he finally stood behind Sarah he reached down to grasp her and was going to turn her around to face him. As he touched her shoulder a severe numbing feeling first spread through his hand and worked its way up his right arm. The numbness changed to pain and quickly spread throughout his body causing him to collapse to the asphalt. In an instant, he perceived that he was bodily removed from his surroundings and placed in some other dimension of existence. But this existence had a very dark side. He immediately understood that he was experiencing hell. As far as his perception could reach, countless millions were subjected to this darkness. He sensed pure remorse and hatred. Next came hopelessness and despair. The evils and disgraceful acts performed against God and man were revealed to him in an endless volley to his mind. Again, and again, the pain and suffering of this forsaken place was manifested to him. Countless souls cried out for relief, but he knew in his heart that none would come. This was the culmination of lifetimes of abuse against each other and the pushing aside of God and his commandments. Bishop Wallace saw the inhumanity of one against the other-the acts of pure hatred and greed. His perception was so real he felt every sin as though it was his own. The sins of murder, adultery, physical and mental abuse, theft and deception exploded in his mind and with each vision also came the face of the victim and the accused. He experienced the pain of the injured, their innocence and betrayal. Next came the emotions at the time of the injustice felt by the sinner, the uncontrollable desire to achieve an end no matter what the cost.

The Bishop could take no more, he cried out for relief from this torture. Within an instant, the images ceased in his mind. He remained in the suffering as an observer but was no longer assailed by the visions. Just as he thought he had the situation under control and could cope with his surroundings, new visions crept into mind, these were of a personal nature and it made him even more uncomfortable then before. These visions were of the injustices he had done to individuals during his lifetime. Each of the faces paraded before him he recognized and with each came the realization of the crime he had committed against them. The merciless acts against his priests just for the sake of flaunting his authority were revealed. Their suffering and his experienced joy seemed to go on endlessly. Next came his supportive staff that he ridiculed and never appreciated. Faces appeared of individuals that sought out his help but instead he turned a deaf ear. Lastly, he became aware of his personal sins of greed, lust for power, overly aggressive ambition and gluttony. The weight of his past sins seemed to press down on him so much so that he felt he would never leave this place and that his final judgment had taken place. Out of desperation and with every breath, he cried out to his God for mercy and compassion. He desired the same mercy and compassion that was lacking in his life.

As his continued pleas left his lips, images of a different nature started to manifest in his immediate surroundings. At first, he was confused but the realization hit him like a ton of bricks. These were the demons that would now take control of his soul and subject him to an eternity of unimaginable pain and suffering for his past sins. All his senses were assailed by these creatures. Their disgusting forms and unimaginable stench made him cower further back into himself. The sounds emanating from their mouths were of an unnatural source and continually echoed throughout his entire being. He cried out again begging for relief and mercy, he didn't want to end his life on earth and spend all of eternity in this forsaken place. If the reward of heaven was being in the presence of God, then hell was truly the absence of God.

As if a light switch was thrown, the darkness and visions disappeared, and he was back in his earthly body. Tears of remorse flowed down his cheeks and for the first time in his life, he truly thanked God for his mercy and forgiveness.

As he became more and more aware of his surrounding, he noticed he still had Sarah by the shoulder. With great effort he raised himself from the asphalt just about the time that Sarah turned to face him. She looked into his eyes and he perceived such a gentleness and warmth from her stare that he wept even more. He released his hold of her shoulder and cupped his face in his hands and wept bitterly for his past sins. All his life had been one staged event after the other; his rise to power, his abusive nature, his lust and greed for the comforts of life. All this time missing the bigger picture by ignoring God and his fellow man. He had the ability and power to help individuals and improve their lives and situations, but he ignored them for his own gain. He felt such sorrow and was repulsed by the man he had become.

Sarah brought the Bishop back to reality by softly calling out his name. He stopped shuddering from the intense remorse to once again look down into her sympathetic eyes. She simply said, "God has forgiven you." He reached down and picked her up and hugged her then placed a simple kiss on her cheek. No further words were needed.

That day, Bishop Wallace changed his life. The very intent of our Lord to change people's behavior so they would follow his commandments and love each other was manifested in him. Sarah had started her public ministry by healing one of the hierarchies of the church. It was not a physical healing, but one of his soul. He would now become a beacon of the love of God and use his position and authority for the honor of God and the betterment of his people. For as long as he was capable, he was steadfast in his support of Sarah and frequently met with her. He often put the resources of the diocese at her disposal for large gatherings and heralded her mission as one from God and assisted in his own way of legitimizing her actions.

Into the evening, as he had time to contemplate his life and the dramatic events of the day, he knew he had to seek forgiveness from those he had injured. God had forgiven him, now he must "settle the score" with man. His first call was to Fr. Mark Wilson. He rationalized that the last to be hurt should be the first to be called.

As Fr. Mark reached for the phone, he noticed the caller ID and shuddered. He assumed the Bishop was calling to gloat about the content of the meeting with Natalie and Sarah and to press forward with another of his power-grabbing agendas. After taking a deep breath he answered the phone.

"Hello, this is Fr. Mark. How may I help you?"

"Fr. Mark, this is Bishop Wallace. How are you? I hope this evening finds you well."

Fr. Mark had never had a conversation start so pleasantly with the Bishop. He couldn't remember the Bishop ever asking how he felt. It was usually right to business which ultimately ended with a scolding for one reason or the other. The Bishop always made him feel like a child being caught in an unforgiveable act. He gained his composure and replied, "I am fine, thank you for asking. So, how did your meeting go with the Martinelli family? I hope and pray your eyes and heart were open to the Spirit and you firmly believe in the authenticity of little Sarah's gift. Tell me, what happened during your visit?"

"Something wonderful," were the only words the Bishop could muster. After a brief pause, he continued. "Fr. Mark, I would like to apologize for the many indiscretions over the years. I know my social skills may not have been up to speed and my lust for power overshadowed my better judgment. You have never been distracted from your priestly role and have supported all my decisions without complaint no matter how ridiculous and self-serving. You have cared for your parishioners with the upmost of sincerity, kindness and support. I honestly can say you are a priest's priest. Please forgive me and pray for me."

Fr. Mark immediately knew that the Bishop had gone through a conversion of his own. Whether it was by the Spirit or as a witness, he knew "something wonderful" had happened.

"Bishop Wallace, there is no need to apologize. I am one of your priests and as such am obedient to your wishes and demands. On occasion, I have had trouble understanding some of your requests, but I feel confident that we have been set on the right path and this is just the start of a revitalization of faith in God. As the news of Sarah's gift spreads and more and more people are witness to her healing graces, we will see a movement like never before to love God and each other and have hope in the future."

"Fr. Mark, I witnessed my own destruction. I witnessed the pain and suffering of people at my hands. I witnessed my eternal damnation. I witnessed hell and all the torment and savagery it conveys. Please believe me when I say that nothing, nothing we ever imagined can equal its reality. It took this experience to soften my heart and open my eyes to what is right and good in the world. I cannot waste this gift and continue down the road to self-destruction. I have seen all that is wrong in the world and I must do all in my power as a leader in the church to change people's actions. I met with Sarah and saw such compassion in her eyes and depth to her love. People must know these things exist. These are the important things that must be nurtured in our lives. The petty squabbling must stop. Once again, everyone must believe in God and obey his commandments. It is the only way to survive this crazy world and obtain our heavenly reward. It can work, but people must be shown the truth. By witnessing the truth, salvation is at hand. It is simple, my eyes have been opened. Now my mission starts."

"I will pray for you more intently now that I know you have found hope in God. You're right in saying it is so simple, love God and love your fellow man. If you obey his two commandments there is no way you would ever commit any offense against God or anybody else. It can truly be a simple way of life to follow. Well, Bishop Wallace, I think I'm going to turn in early this evening. With the lack of pain from my previous ailments and my newfound energy, I try to accomplish too much each day and I still get tired at night. Please forgive me if I have to go now."

"This has been a wonderful conversation for me and I hope it was for you too. If you don't mind I would like to drop by from time to time for a visit just to chat. I hear your garden is always the envy of others. I must try some of your vegetables. Please have a peaceful rest and God bless and protect you."

"The same to you, Bishop Wallace."

The Bishop made numerous calls that evening to right the many wrongs he had committed. Priests and the laity alike were at first shocked at his pleas for forgiveness, then experienced a healing of their own. When they understood how Bishop Wallace's conversion had occurred they were moved by the Spirit in their own way. The content of his comforting words seemed to ignite a fire in their hearts. A cloud that had obscured the truth from their eyes was whisked away by the gentle breeze of love and compassion. The simple words from a truly penitent man made the difference in their lives. These emotions, these feelings, these truths would begin to resonate from individual to individual in a never-ending domino effect, all initiated by a man seeking forgiveness.

For many days Bishop Wallace would attempt to reach out to those he had hurt or neglected in the past, either by phone or personal visit. When he was satisfied he had done his best to correct his past mistakes, he started his own mission. With great zeal and a clear vision of what must be accomplished he used all the various forms of media at his disposal to begin his work. Articles were written each week for the local religious paper and he bought space in the local newspapers to reach as many as possible. Interviews were given on the radio and TV, some of which were picked-up by the national stations. He abandoned the daily drudgery of administration and became a modern-day St. Paul, preaching and spreading the good news. His experiences and position in the church made him a reliable source that legitimized this new-found faith, hope and love that was spreading like a wildfire. He felt good about himself and knew he was truly going about God's business. From time to time he would contemplate his journey to hell and back. He would shudder to think that that could have been his ultimate damnation for all of eternity. But every day he went down on bended knee to thank God for his conversion and to pray for Sarah's safety and success. He would die a happy person in the eyes of God and man.

Chapter 4

Sarah continued to reach out to as many of the faithful as possible during her first day of public ministry. She encountered people from all walks of life that believed in God and she prayed for relief of their physical afflictions. Men and women of all ages flocked to her, just to be touched. The curing continued as promised by God.

The majority that presented themselves to Sarah that first day lived relatively close to her, but the word was spreading. Virtually everyone on the planet who had access to a televised medium or the Internet had now seen the remarkable interview from the evening before and many started their own pilgrimage to Sarah's home town. It was just a matter of time before arrangements would have to be made on a grand scale to place Sarah in a massive arena setting that could accommodate the wave after wave of people seeking her help.

When physical exhaustion had finally overcome her ability to function at a level that she felt comfortable, Sarah decided to end her work for the day. The gathered crowd understood and parted from her immediate space and allowed her to make her way back to the solitude of her home. Natalie was there at the top of the steps to greet her; she had hardly moved all day. The two of them wished those still gathered a good evening and asked God's blessing for them and promised they would be available bright and early the next day. With that farewell, they retired inside of their home.

Natalie scooped up Sarah into her arms and kissed her gently on the cheek. They stayed together in a hug until Natalie felt Sarah go limp in her arms. She carried her up the stairs and into her bedroom. As she made her way up the stairs she reminisced of Sarah's early childhood and the countless nights that she had carried Sarah to her bedroom in like manner. She longed for those simpler times when it was just the two of them, no crowds, no reporters, nothing in their lives but the two of them. They were difficult times, having to raise Sarah without her father in her life, always trying to make ends meet, too much month left at the end of the paycheck. Trying to be both mother and father to her and trying to make sure she had a stable life had been a major undertaking. She always doubted herself but found hope in her daily prayers and seeing the ever-present sparkle in little Sarah's eyes. Natalie knew she had done a good job and thanked God for their many blessings.

While still holding Sarah, Natalie pulled down the comforter and top sheet from her bed. She gently laid Sarah down and removed her outer clothing then covered her with the top sheet. The daily shower could wait until the morning, what was needed now was undisturbed sleep. Natalie bent down and kissed her little angel goodnight then closed the door behind her. She went through the house making sure all the doors and windows were secure then turned out all the lights. She retired to her bedroom and completed her nightly ritual to prepare for bed herself. She normally read or watched the evening news but that was not the case tonight. Any novel she was engrossed in could wait for another day and she knew the news would be completed dominated by Sarah and her mission. Sleep was more important. She rolled over, turned the lamp off and prayed for a speedy release from the happenings of the day. Her prayers were answered.

Over the next few nights as Sarah was enveloped in a deep sleep, many early saints and martyrs of the church visited her in her dreams. She realized the need for her second gift of wisdom and understanding and marveled at the intense love of God that these nightly visitors possessed. Saint Stephen was the first to come to her. He was the first to die for his faith in the early church. He relayed his experiences of being a deacon and teaching God's word. Ultimately, the enemies of the church of Jesus plotted against him and eventually stoned him to death for his beliefs. She conversed with him and found great insight into understanding the zeal this early convert had for Jesus and his new religion.

As Saint Stephen vanished Saints Peter and Paul appeared. This dynamic duo was so excited to be with her she couldn't get them to leave. They seemed to be in competition for her attention and touted their actions and achievements after their conversion. Saint Paul was definitely the greater speaker of the two, but Saint Peter had a charm that Sarah couldn't resist. Some of the other original apostles visited her as well and she was equally inspired by their talks. Next appeared other saints who are considered the great doctors or teachers of the church. Saint Hilary of Poitiers, Saint Cyril of Jerusalem, Saint Gregory the Great, Saint Jerome, Saint Augustine, Saint Bede, Saint Thomas Quinoas, Saint Catherine of Siena and Saint Teresa of Avila all made their presence known and helped Sarah understand and better comprehend the teachings of the church that she so loved. The last group to visit Sarah was Saint John Bosco, Saint Elizabeth Anne Seton and Saint John Neumann. These were the modern-day saints that gave an insight into the relatively recent period of the church and its teachings. She felt closeness to them that she hadn't experienced with her previous visitors.

As she closed this chapter of her mission, Sarah knew why God had allowed these nightly visits and the impact they would have on her future endeavors. God wanted her to be successful and afforded her with all the necessary skills and information to be so. She marveled at their lives and the internal strength it required for them to have such faith and conviction. She would summon every ounce of strength to emulate these great men and women. These encounters would not be wasted on her.

Day two seemed to appear out of the midst of Sarah's subconscious with little time to savor the successes of the previous day. Natalie was already sitting on the edge of her bed and just stared down at her. "Oh Mom, what's up? How did I get into my bed last night? I remember coming into the house and us hugging but that was it."

"You were physically and emotionally drained, so I put you to bed myself. Why don't you take a shower and we'll see what today has in store for us?"

"Mom, I had some of the most amazing visitors appear in my dreams last night. Some of the early saints and martyrs came and spent time with me. Jesus wants me to have a thorough understanding of my faith and how the church developed here on earth after he went to heaven. I can't begin to explain how fascinating these people were and how sincere and profound they are in their beliefs."

"I don't think we can ever be surprised again after what we've gone through in such a short period of time. God chose you for his own reasons and has given you all the skills and knowledge you need to successfully complete your mission. He has a grand plan and we don't know what that plan is just yet. But I'm sure you'll be the first to know."

"I'll do as I'm instructed, Mom, and besides, with you at my side I can't fail, I never have with you there supporting me in the past. I don't know how this will all work out, but I must tell you I'm so glad you are here with me. You have been the perfect role model for me all these years and have always supported me in all that I attempted to accomplish. You were both mother and father to me and I never wanted for anything. I love you so much. You can't imagine how grateful I am for you in my life."

At that instance a ripple or wave or chill ran through Natalie's body. She couldn't describe it; she had never experienced anything like it before. She finally realized the nature of the effect, it was her complete happiness in the love for her daughter and the pride that she felt for raising such a remarkable person and having that love returned. She could only say, "I love you too." That was all that was needed.

Natalie peeked through the blinds on one of the windows that faced the street. As far as the eye could see in every direction, people were assembled waiting for their potential healer. Natalie felt an apprehension in her heart for her daughter. This was only day two and already an incalculable number of people were here to be touched by Sarah and hopefully experience their own miracle. How was her daughter to survive day after day under these conditions? What kind of life would this be for her? Like all parents, Natalie hoped someday Sarah would find the man of her dreams and settle down to raise a family of her own. She wanted nothing more than to have a strong man in Sarah's life that she so sorely missed by not having a father. Natalie wanted the joy of someday having a grandchild to hold and love just as she did with Sarah. To have the bottles and diapers again throughout the house, the daily baths of an infant, the cuddling and fresh smell of a newborn, was this too much to ask? After all, Sarah had been cheated out of a normal life with the lack of the influence of a father. Why was she chosen? Why was Sarah's life the life that would be devoid of this happiness? Natalie found herself sinking into a deep state of depression. She had never felt like this before. Even after Michael was gone, she found great comfort and joy in raising Sarah.

Natalie came to the realization that there were evil entities at work here attempting to corrupt the sacred nature of Sarah's gifts. She knew that if an evil force could somehow get to her, Sarah would sense the change and be adversely affected. She could not let this happen. The love of her daughter would not allow her own fears and shortcomings to counter everything that Sarah had worked for and achieved. The more Natalie became aware of this negative force the stronger it got. Internally, she felt all that she held dear struggling against the evil of depression and despair. She had to fight it off. She had to be victorious. She couldn't let Sarah know about this weakness within her. The only thing she could do was pray and pray as never before. She prayed for relief and strength and the will to conquer this evil presence. She felt the sweat streaming down her brow as the will to beat this negativity increased. Just as the dark pain within her seemed to be gaining momentum, it abruptly halted, and she found relief. She gasped as the tension in her body eased and her heartbeat became regular again. From deep inside she heard these words, "Peace be unto you my child." At that moment Natalie knew her prayers were answered and that she had heard the voice of God. Happiness spread over her and she understood how Sarah must have felt when she first heard God's voice and was later in his presence. With this newfound strength, Natalie understood the destructive power of this evil force. She felt confident she now had the ability to counter its effects in the future and would never allow it to control her again.

Sarah came next to her and looked out of the window at the crowd below. "Looks like another busy day going about the Lord's business," she said. Both burst into a heavy laugh at that understatement. "We better get started," said Natalie.

Sarah and Natalie both took their showers and then dressed into something comfortable. They met at the top of the stairs and were ready to make the trip down when Natalie said, "Hey, what are we going to do about school? Don't forget you are only eleven and have quite a few years of education ahead of you."

"Mom, I have been given many special gifts from God and He has told me there are more to come. I really don't think that my worldly education can in anyway match what I have learned and will learn from God. I think it is a moot point."

"My, my, such clarity and at such an early age." They both laughed again and headed down the steps, hand in hand.

Natalie was about to suggest something for breakfast. She felt guilty that Sarah hadn't eaten well yesterday and was determined that would not be the case today. Suddenly, there was a hard banging on the front door. It was three fast and hard knocks and then silence. Natalie just figured that it was one of the impatient faithful that wanted to be first this day, so she approached and opened the door. The faithful were all still gathered in the surrounding streets and no one was on the porch. As she further surveyed the immediate area she glanced down and at first, she thought her eyes were playing tricks on her. On the porch to the side was set up a table with two chairs. The table was covered with the most beautiful satin cloth with matching napkins. Lead crystal goblets and glasses were filled with water and orange juice and fine china and silverware were precisely arranged as if on a picture in a high-end food magazine. Covered chafing dishes surrounded a beautiful bouquet of flowers that occupied the center of the table. Natalie shook her head in disbelief and raised her glance to look at the people in the street. As her eyes met theirs an unbelievable thing happened, all the people at once stated to clap their hands and yell shouts of joy in her direction. She didn't know what to make of it. Hearing the revelry, Sarah joined her mom and was overwhelmed at the sight. They stood there for some time in gratitude of the appreciation shown them. After a while Natalie raised her hands. They immediately responded with their silence. She felt it important to address the crowd.

"Sarah and I want to thank you for respecting our privacy last night and for your most warm greeting this morning. We know many of you are from the local area and many have arrived here after traveling some distance. I can assure you that we will do everything in our power to make your encounter here one of joy and enrichment. Hopefully, also one of healing."

She continued, "I don't know who the benefactor was of this beautiful breakfast spread but it is greatly appreciated and will definitely be enjoyed." Many in the crowd laughed at that comment. "If you will excuse us, we can eat our breakfast and Sarah will then be down to meet and pray with you".

Natalie and Sarah took seats at the table which was just to the side of the steps on the porch. The brick railing was adequately in height, so they could eat without seeing the stares from the crowd. But that wasn't the case. The assembled masses turned away from their home to afford them as much privacy as possible.

Each dish was uncovered to reveal cuisine for which any chef would be happy to take credit. Eggs Benedict, French toast, blueberry pancakes, bacon, sausage patties and home fries were proudly presented with all the accompanying preserves and syrups. A finely-crafted silver carafe finished the setting which Natalie knew would contain a superior blend of coffee, one of her few vices. At first, Natalie and Sarah could only stare at each dish as it was uncovered. But as if on cue they each thought, that's enough of the savoring, let's eat! It was truly a meal fit for a king.

At first, there was little conversation at the table. The tastes from each entree exploded in their mouths as they retrieved and sampled each of the offerings. The meal was truly heavenly, which brought them both to the realization that they didn't know the source of the food. But their ravenous appetites kept them focused on the consumption of the many gifts spread before them and they soon forgot about any of the nagging questions still unanswered.

As the appetites were satisfied and the tummies were full, they both pushed slightly away from the table and decided to have a little conversation and bonding time. With all that had happened over the last few days, there had been very little time left just for them. Throughout her short existence, Sarah had always enjoyed the down time spent with her mother and hoped that would never change.

"I was wondering, Sarah, and I'm sure you were too, who placed this fantastic breakfast on our porch? It was as though someone read our minds or heard our thoughts and acted on our needs. Don't you think that was strange?"

"I can't say, Mom, but it does seem strange."

"There is a verse in the bible in the gospel of Saint Mark that reflects on the instructions given to the disciples by Jesus as they started their public ministries." Curiosity got the better of Natalie and she had to know what was said in the passage. She knew it had some relevance to this situation. She got up from the table and ran into the house to retrieve their family bible. She returned to the porch and continued to flip pages until she arrived at the gospel of Mark and found the desired verses. She read aloud, "***These were his instructions: 'Take nothing for the journey except a staff—no bread, no bag, no money in your belts. Wear sandals but not an extra tunic. Whenever you enter a house, stay there until you leave that town. And if any place will not***

***welcome you or listen to you, shake the dust off your feet when you leave, as a testimony against them'"*.**

"I believe in my heart that somehow these words have a direct bearing on how we are to conduct our lives while you fulfill your ministry. The disciples needed nothing but the clothes on their backs as they traveled from town to town spreading the news of God's love and performing miracles. It appears you're a modern-day disciple of God and I believe this is how we must deal with our physical needs. I feel that all we need will be given to us out of sincere appreciation for the healing graces you are offering to God's children. Look at this breakfast. Where did it come from? How was it placed on our porch just as we were talking about finding something to eat this morning? If I am to be here to watch over you, how can I return to work and earn an income to keep this house going?" Natalie stopped the flow of questions waiting for some type of response from Sarah. She finally spoke.

"I think your interpretation is correct. We must be about the Lord's business and concentrate solely on my mission. Who knows what's in store for us on a day to day basis, so I believe it is a fair assumption that we will have to rely on the goodness and generosity of those we help. Let's just see how things go over the next few days."

"I have a lot of vacation and personal days left on the books at work, so I'll call in today and request the next week off. We'll see what happens after that."

Natalie and Sarah's assumptions were correct. For as long as they remained in their home, each day at least three meals would appear on their porch just at the right time. The mortgage on their home somehow was paid-off. None of the other usual statements from the utility companies or even annual taxes were ever received again in their mail. Natalie stopped worrying after the first few months when the bills didn't arrive. At first, she made inquiries but was always told that the bills were taken care of by anonymous individuals who didn't want their identity known. So, she figured that this was one less thing to be concerned over.

Natalie and Sarah afforded themselves a few more minutes of quiet time together as Natalie finished her second cup of coffee. With a mutual smile they got up from the table, hugged each other and Sarah walked down the steps to the eagerly waiting masses. Like bees surrounding their queen, the crowd moved in around Sarah and her ministry began.

Chapter 5

Rocco lifted the baseball bat high into the air and allowed his eyes to follow its contours from top to bottom. He took in all its magnificence. This was his favorite tool in his arsenal of weapons. The bat was made of aluminum. He loved the sound generated when it made contact. The weight had to be thirty-two ounces and the length thirty-five inches. Over time he found this to be the best fit for his grip and the best weight to develop the maximum impact.

Rocco looked down into the fear-filled eyes of his latest victim. Weasel was in a tough bind and had turned to Rocco for relief from his other underworld creditors. But Weasel thought his trips to the track and other numbers schemes would pay off in time to repay Rocco with the exorbitant interest included. He was wrong. Everything he touched turned against him and now it was time to pay up. He had already gotten two payback extensions from Rocco which also included additional heavy percentages of interest.

Rocco had to track him down which just angered him even more. When Weasel said he didn't have the money, Rocco dragged him into this alley, opened the trunk of his car and showed Weasel his assortment of final collection devices. Weasel went into a litany of excuses and pleas for mercy and requested another extension, but Rocco wouldn't hear of it. His policy was never to exceed two extensions, it was just bad business. So here was Weasel lying on the ground with Rocco's size thirteen left boot holding his neck and head to the ground. Rocco took a few practice swings then came around with the bat and struck Weasel directly in the left temple. The metallic sound echoed off the surrounding brick walls. Fragments of hair, tissue and bone flew into the air from the impact sight. Crimson red blood spewed from the wound and started a river of red rippling between the bricks and down toward an open drain. Weasel's cranium was snapped from his neck and spine and lay limp and motionless, barely attached to the trunk of his body.

Rocco stepped off the torn neck and moved so he could stand directly above Weasel. Rocco next lowered the bat, so it was against Weasel's face. Then using the bat like a golf club, he went into his back swing and brought the bat down directly into Weasel's face. His tremendous strength and accuracy left little of Weasel's face intact. Rocco laughed to himself. He couldn't quite decide whether the initial baseball style swing or the follow-up golf swing was his favorite; they both made that wonderful metallic sound from the bat. Oh well, he got his point across to Weasel. This form of punishment would make others think twice before they delayed or neglected to repay him in the agreed timeframe.

Rocco rummaged through his truck and found a roll of paper towels. He ripped off a bunch of sheets and began to clean the baseball bat with a bottle of water and the towels. He wasn't worried about the blood or tissue clinging to its surface but rather his finger prints. After multiple cleanings, he tossed the bat into the air which landed about five feet from Weasel's body. Rocco slammed shut the trunk lid, slipped behind the wheel and drove out of the alleyway. This was his last stop for the day and he decided to head directly home to check on his mother.

Rocco's mother, Vivian, was up in age and was burdened with Alzheimer's disease. Over the last three years he could do nothing but stand by and watch her lose one body function after another. It saddened him that she barely recognized him anymore. His mom was the only parent in his life from the age of eleven. He had lost his dad at an early age due to his involvement with organized crime. Rocco followed in his father's footsteps. He easily rose through the ranks of his underworld companions by never stepping on anyone's toes and always forming the right alliances. Now he pretty much answered to no one. He had used his resources wisely and converted his illegitimate earnings into legitimate, sound investments and built quite a substantial collection of successful businesses. With all his perceived power and wealth, he could do nothing to slow or halt the progress of his mother's disease.

He made his way through the winding roads of his neighborhood with its well-manicured lawns and luxurious mansions. The exterior lights were just beginning to come on which enhanced the beauty of the magnificent buildings. Rocco arrived at his front gate and pressed the center button on the garage opener and the iron gate slid sideways. He drove up the cobblestone driveway and pulled his car into an open bay in his cavernous garage. Rocco bounded up the stairs and into the kitchen area of his house. The nurse who was on duty for this eight-hour shift was in the kitchen preparing a light snack for his mom. He exchanged pleasantries with her and inquired into the type of day his mom had. She offered much the same report that he received every other day, pretty much no change. For the most part he always took that as a good report. He walked past her and made his way through the grand house and up the main staircase to his mom's bedroom. He found her sitting in a wheel chair staring out of the massive bay window which dominated the large wall facing the back of the estate. He approached her slowly. She was skittish, and he hated it when she got startled. He crossed around to face her and leaned over to kiss her cheek. He never knew how she would respond to his greeting. This time he was relieved to see the sense of recognition in her face and the smile that spread over her lips.

"Hi dear, when did you get home?"

"Just a couple of minutes ago," he said. "How are you feeling?"

"Just great, no aches or pains today. Where is Jennifer?"

"Norma in on duty now and she is in the kitchen fixing your snack. What did you tell her to make for you?"

"I think you're mistaking dear, Jennifer is on duty now. I just spent the last hour with her and told her to make me a snack. Is your father home yet?"

Damn it, he thought to himself, he lost her again. He knew from experience she was now gone, and it would be fruitless to try and have a meaningful conversation with her.

He searched the room for the TV remote control and found it on the nightstand next to his mother's bed. He retrieved it then pressed the ON button and the required buttons to tune in the nightly news. The reporter was delivering a story about a small girl that was some type of a faith healer. Yeah, right. What a gimmick, he thought. He changed channels and there appeared another reporter delivering the same story. Now his interest was piqued. He sat on the edge of the bed and listened to the story. He got so engrossed with what he was hearing that he had to increase the volume.

From what he could tell by the reporter's excited tone, a local young girl was healing people of their physical afflictions and doing so from the street in front of her home. The reporter went on to say that the local Bishop and a priest also had some type of a healing experience during their encounter with her. The cameraman working with the reporter panned the crowd which surrounded the girl. She seemed to be walking through their midst with her eyes lowered. She stopped at each one and laid her hands on them. Some were on crutches, others in wheelchairs, still others were lying on gurneys. Each of these individuals had one or two people assisting them to obtain access to the girl. Rocco watched intently the results of her touch. As she released her touch of the afflicted, there seemed to occur a change over them, some type of an enlightenment. Then the strangest thing happened most of time. The individual that was just touched by the girl seemed to be cured of their affliction. People removed the crutches from under their arms and simply walked away. Others who were previously confined to a wheelchair got up and pushed the wheelchair out of the crowded area. Even those on the gurneys were able to step off the portable bed and walk away on their own power.

Rocco had trouble believing his eyes and ears. He thought to himself, is this real or one of the biggest scams in history? It couldn't be a scam, too many people are involved. Could he use this girl to cure his mother? Then he noticed that some of the people approaching the girl weren't being cured. What was that all about? Then he noticed something posted on the bottom of the screen. The girl's address was displayed for everyone to see. It was like they were inviting everyone to have a shot at her healing powers. What a bunch of schmucks. If she was savvy she'd have somebody following her and demanding payment for her services. Oh well, there's a sucker born every minute, he thought. He devised a plan to take his mother there in the morning to see if she would be one of the lucky ones that got cured. At this point, he was willing to try anything to reverse the symptoms of her disease.

The alarm went off at 5:30 AM the next morning. Rocco wanted to get there early so he didn't have to wait long and cause his mother any unnecessary discomfort. By the time Rocco had showered and dressed, the night nurse had his mother ready to make the trip. Rocco had pulled his large SUV to the front entrance and went to retrieve his mother. The nurse accompanied Rocco as he pushed his mother in her wheelchair into the elevator. He pressed the button for the lowest level of his home. The doors closed, and the sound of the motor could be heard as the elevator car was lowered the two floors. Once outside, the nurse helped Rocco situate his mother in the front passenger seat. The nurse was about to get into the back seat when Rocco stopped her. He insisted that he could handle her for the rest of the day and told her she could either finish her shift in the house or take an early leave and go home. He had left instructions with the nursing agency that his mother may not be home for the next shift change but that the nurse should still wait at the house for his mother's return. He thought to himself, this may not work, and I'll need somebody at the house to supply my mother with her usual care.

Rocco pulled the SUV out of the driveway and steered the behemoth vehicle in the direction of the address that was indicated on the TV last night. As he drove, conflicting thoughts ran through his mind. He tried to sort through what he had seen on the news report. Would this really work, or would it be a disappointment? He didn't think his mother had any idea of what was going on and why they were making this early morning trip into a strange neighborhood. It was up to him to explore any possible avenue of cure for his mother, it was his ultimate responsibility. She had dedicated her life to him as a single parent, now he had to repay her lifelong kindnesses. She had never dated anyone or would never have considered marrying anyone after the loss of her husband. The raising of her son was of paramount importance and she always felt she had done a pretty good job. Look at how successful a business man he was. She was totally ignorant to the facts of his underworld involvement. She considered him a model citizen and was very proud of how he turned out and subconsciously took most of the credit for his success.

As Rocco read the directions given on his navigation system, he failed to see the crowds already assembled three blocks away from his intended destination. He had to slam on the brakes of the SUV to avoid running into the outermost ring of the faithful. He swore so loudly that it startled his mother out of a sleepy trance. She said, "What was that dear?"

"Nothing, Mother, I just have to find us a parking place near here."

"Where are we going?" she said. "None of this looks familiar to me."

"Don't worry, I have everything under control. There's someone you need to meet, and she is near here."

"Are we going to have breakfast? I haven't eaten yet and am hungry."

"No Mom, you already had your breakfast before we left the house."

"What time is it? Did your dad leave for work?"

"Yes, Mom, he left before we did."

Rocco found it easy just to play along with his mother when she slipped into these forgetful periods. It saved him the aggravation of repeating himself, and he felt it was less stressful for his mom.

Rocco had to back out of the street and drive an additional two blocks to find a parking space that would accommodate the SUV. He retrieved the wheelchair from the back seat then opened the passenger door. He reached in and picked up his mother and gently placed her in the familiar space of the chair. After hitting the lock button on the vehicle's key fob, he started to wheel his mother back in the direction of the little girl's home. As he worked his way down the street, more and more people started to arrive, and his intended route became congested. Then everything came to halt. He figured he was still at least four city blocks from the house and based on the people in front of him he doubted if he would even make it there by the end of the day.

As usual, nothing ever deterred Rocco from any of his objectives so mentally he devised a system. Although in some type of a makeshift queue, people never really stood still, they shifted back and forth from side to side to ease the pressure and weight on each leg. He observed this behavior and would use it to his advantage. As individuals moved he pushed the wheelchair containing his mom into the slightly open gap. When people shifted back they would bump into the wheelchair and be unset that they had possibly disturbed or even worse, hurt the poor, frail senior in the chair. Immediate, "I'm sorry" and "Oh, please, forgive me" would flow with total sincerity in their voices. Depending on his mood at the time, Rocco would issue either "No problem" or "That's okay" or he would take the alternate approach and issue a sever-looking glance.

His system was working and within two hours he was within visual range of the girl. During this two-hour, slow-paced trek, the thing that amazed him the most was the peace that seemed to permeate the area. He was witness to many large gatherings in the past such as sporting events, concerts and even navigating the downtown metropolitan area. People were rude, loud and had no concern for others. But here, people seemed to care for the plight of their fellow journeymen. Rest stations, many with first aid services, were placed along the route and free water was available at every turn. Rocco wondered who was footing the bill for all of this and how it got organized so quickly. From his understanding, this was only the third day that this girl was in the streets outside of her home. Again, some schmuck must have been suckered into footing the bill for all these services.

Because of his considerable height, Rocco was able to scan the area to see how close he was to the girl and if there was a better avenue to make his approach. That's when he noticed a large exit corridor that was set up to move people away from the girl after their encounter. As people were touched by her, they moved to the open area to allow the next group access to the girl. He did his usual maneuvering and soon found himself having access to the open route. He lifted the flimsy rope that sectioned off the route over his head then with his mother in tow, slipped under the restraint. Now free of the crowd, he covered the short distance to the girl with ease. Nobody stopped him or even put up an objection. What a bunch of weaklings, he thought. You can walk all over people and never get a rise out of them.

There she was and just a few feet away. His mother's cure was just a couple of steps away and he would be out of here and back home within an hour. He started to formulate an exit plan that would easily take him through the crowd when his eyes suddenly fell upon the girl's face. At first, he marveled at her simple beauty then realized he was staring at a very young girl. He thought he remembered the reporter saying she was only eleven years old. But her actions and intensity of purpose belied her true age. With undiminished energy she reached out to each person and seemed to be there just for them at that moment. She touched them on the arm or cupped their head in her hands while bowing her head and mumbling something. The encounter was over in seconds but the joy and peace that he witnessed spreading across the recipient's faces should have taken a lifetime to accumulate. Maybe this is the real thing, he thought. Maybe this is my mother's lucky day after all.

A young boy in a wheelchair was the last obstacle blocking his access to the girl. This kid was pretty messed up. From the looks of it he must have been in a very bad accident. He was covered from head to toe in different casts. Pins protruded from both the casts on his legs and some type of a wire halo surrounded his head. I sure wouldn't want to be the guy who hit him and have that liability. Rocco assumed this was the result of an automobile accident.

The girl did her usual thing by touching the boy's shoulder and mumbling something. When she let go he raised his head and smiled at her. He asked his dad to help him out of the wheelchair. His dad came around to face him. He dropped the two wheelchair supports that held his legs straight and reached down to help get him out of the chair. Guessing that the kid couldn't stand all that stuff against his body, he started to rip everything off. The wire halo was the first to go, then the cast on his left arm then one after the other, he removed the leg casts. Even though pins had protruded through the casts and into his bones, everything came off and there was no visible sign of any wounds or scars on his legs. Because of the boy's insistence that all his hardware be removed, the girl had to linger a little longer in his area. The boy ran over to her and hugged her and thanked her repeatedly. The father next came to her and hugged her. He then attempted to force her to take something from him. It was a standard white envelope, but it looked very thick. Rocco overheard her sternly refuse to take the envelope and said all he should do is pray for her. The father stopped pressuring her and simply shook his head up and down in agreement. He and his son collected all the medical supplies that were scattered about and stacked them on the wheelchair. The father pushed the wheelchair and the two of them left with the boy hanging his arm around his dad's waist.

As Rocco wheeled his mother closer to the girl, she turned and this time their eyes met. Rocco had to stop in his tracks. His legs refused to move and obey his mental commands. Her stare reached past any visual state and burrowed deep into his very being. He had never experienced anything like this before. He was totally mesmerized and was completely helpless. He was aware that she was approaching him but could do nothing to move away. She was a little girl, but she had control over him to the point that for the first time in a long time he felt threatened.

"Do you know why you are here today?" she said. "You may think you are in control but don't kid yourself with such false bravado." The girl moved closer and took his hand. Instantly, a shockwave rippled throughout his body that caused him to bend over in pain. The pain increased until he could bear it no longer and he collapsed to the street. The girl still had hold of his hand and he struggled to break free but couldn't. As she held his hand, he sensed a transfer of some sort. He couldn't decide if it was information in its purest form or visions in an endless volley overloading all his senses. The first things to register were the memories of his early childhood, the love he had for his dad and the things they enjoyed doing together. His trips to the country where he and his dad would fish until the evening hours flashed before him and he longed for those simple days once again.

The stack upon stack of wrapped gifts from the many childhood Christmases next came into view and he pondered the generosity of his father. Rocco didn't consider the source of the gifts but subconsciously he knew they were obtained by illegal means. He then revisited the night his dad was killed by the police. Rocco's father was involved in a shootout trying to escape from a late-night warehouse heist. It was not only the loss of his father but the humiliation he had to bear for the next couple of years that made him bitter in life. The faces of his many victims next appeared. The first was when he was only sixteen. He decided that day to follow in his father's footsteps but to be overly cautious and not make any stupid mistakes. Many of his victims ended up as Weasel but not all. Some were simply cheated out of something that Rocco badly wanted and he would stop at nothing to get.

Not all the remaining visions were of a dark nature. Rocco saw the great joy he brought to his mother's life and the immeasurable pride she had in him. He kept his criminal side from her and was thankful that she had such high regard for him.

The visions came suddenly to an abrupt end, and a void formed in his subconscious. This void or darkness seemed to linger which made Rocco tense and irritated. Suddenly, the darkness was replaced by an ever-increasing brilliant light. It continued to grow in intensity until there materialized in its midst a figure that he only recently got to know. It was the girl. She spoke to him in a soft tone but with authority.

"My name is Sarah. Now that we have been introduced you can stop referring to me as the girl." She continued. "I have been given a very special gift from God and as such it must be treated with the upmost of respect. The way you made your way through the crowd today doesn't show respect to this gift or to my ministry. You used intelligence and deception to snake your way to me with absolutely no regard for all the other suffering people around you. Do you wonder why these people didn't object to your tactics? It's because they have love in their hearts. They took sympathy on your mom and on her condition. They didn't question why or how their encounter with your mom happened. They felt compassion for her plight and didn't object to your aggressiveness even if it meant the delay in their own healing. As for the water and first aid stations, these were setup by volunteers. People who want to make a difference in the world.

"I never knew my dad, he was killed in the first gulf war. But look at my life and what I have become. I had the free will to grow up either with a chip on my shoulder and anger in my heart or to appreciate the loving mother I had who made every sacrifice for me. I chose the latter. Now I am eleven years old and have had to assume this adult role which I gladly did. You at least had your dad for eleven years but decided to follow a different path. Why? You had a loving mother that did everything for you. Like my mother she longed to have a masculine figure in your life. Your dad made some bad choices and removed himself from the equation. So, she took on the role of both parents and loved and nurtured you. You appreciated what she did for you and always cared for her. You see, that is the dilemma here. You care so much for one person but disregard the sacredness of life of others. Life is a gift, a gift from God. He commands all the universe, and in his love and mercy created man to share these wonderful resources. All He ever asked of us was to love Him and each other. But many people such as you flagrantly disregard the sacredness of life and stop at nothing to amass vast amounts of power and material riches. If someone is hurt or destroyed in the process, it's of no consequence to you. This is one of the main reasons why I was given my special gift. It was to prove to all mankind that God exists, loves us and wants us to obtain eternal life in Him.

"You have accumulated many resources but when is enough, enough? You have converted your ill-gained largesse to legitimate businesses and investments to the point you appear on paper to be a respectable businessman. But look at the cost. How many lives have you destroyed? How many people have been eliminated to help build your empire?"

Rocco could not come up with a response to Sarah. Every word coming from her mouth was the truth and it made him cower under its weight. For the first time his life was exposed for what it truly was, one of deceit, lies and murder all for the accumulation of wealth. Pursuit of the almighty dollar had been the only driving force in his life. It blinded him to the riches in life that can't be bought with money. He never married or had kids, refused to have any contact with other family members, didn't get involved with church or community organizations. Because of his involvement in crime, he felt it was better to have as few people in his life as possible, the only exception was his mother.

Now his soul was laid bare before this young girl. He knew his way of life was over. His mother would be made aware of his past indiscretions and it would break her heart. The years of lies would now come back to haunt him. He anticipated the agonizing look of disappointment in his mother's eyes and knew it would be too much for her to bear. Why did he come here today? Why would his mother be cured now that his plot was uncovered? Countless questions ran through his mind with increasing madness until at last he heard a comforting voice.

"Rocco be at peace. You have seen many glimpses of your life, some good but most were bad. You have been given a chance to correct these misdeeds and save your immortal soul. Many coming here have a physical healing but yours is one of a spiritual nature. Out of compassion you brought your mother here for her own curing, she will obtain it. But unbeknownst to you this was a saving journey of a sort for you. You would not have come here today if you did not have the love for your mother. You would have looked on the news story last night as a big hoax and continued toward the path to destruction. But inadvertently, by wanting to help your mother no matter the cost or effort, you have saved yourself."

Sarah released Rocco's hand and instantly, he was removed from the pure light and became aware of his presence in the crowded street. Looking up he was at eye level with Sarah. She reached out and offered him a hand which he accepted. He rose from his knees and once again towered over Sarah. He looked down at her and remained speechless. What words can a reformed sinner of his kind speak at this moment, he thought. A sense of remorse came over his face, altering its appearance. Deep lines appeared in his cheeks and a grey paleness altered his flesh tone. He was truly sorry for his past sins and wanted desperately to obtain forgiveness.

Sensing the change in Rocco, Sarah reached up and took his hand once again. This time there was no pain, only warmth. This time there were no terrible glimpses into his past sins, only the sight of this little angel standing before him. Rocco lost it at that moment and wept bitterly. He finally understood what Sarah meant when she said our God was a loving God and wanted us to have eternal life in him. He was getting a second chance, something that he never afforded any of his victims. Sarah got him to calm down and said, "Now let's tend to your mother."

Rocco wiped the tears from his eyes enough to watch what happened next. Sarah walked over to face his mother. Vivian looked up and smiled at Sarah, but the smile was one of vagueness and incomprehension. Sarah placed her hand on Vivian's forehead and began to pray. Vivian became aware of Sarah's prayer and joined in praying the Our Father. When they were done, a broad smile spread over Vivian's face. She looked up at Sarah and said, "Those beautiful words were lost to me for so many years. Hearing you pray them released me from my prison and I had to pray them with you. Who are you and how did I get here?"

Rocco was behind his mother, so she was completely confused. He walked over to face her and asked her if she could stand. Without hesitation, Vivian rose from her wheelchair and stood before her son. She reached out and hugged Rocco with total recognition of who he was. She released her hug and stepped back to look at her son. Instantly, the grave lines in his face and grey paleness of his complexion disappeared to reveal a youthful son, the son that Vivian remembered.

Rocco looked at Sarah and said, "Well, now what?"

"That's up to you. You have free will to fall back into your past life or become something that your mother can truly be proud of. The choice is yours."

"I'll take the latter," he said.

Rocco bent over and kissed Sarah on the top of her head. A simple thank you and your welcome were exchanged. With his arm under his mother's, Rocco left the area to start a new life.

As they were walking the few blocks back to his SUV, Vivian inquired what Sarah meant by "your past life," and "something your mother can be proud of?"

Rocco gave out a nervous laugh and told his mother he would explain that some other time. He was grateful Vivian hadn't become aware of his past sins and continued to hold him is such high regard. From now on, he would make his mother happy. With the withdrawal from his ways of crime, he started to lead a normal life. He started dating and eventually found his soulmate and was married. To further fulfill his life, he and his wife started a family. Initially, Rocco was ill-at-ease with the thought of being a father, it all was so foreign to him. Eventually, the daily routine of diaper changing and 2 o'clock feedings became normal for him so-much-so that he looked forward to the chores. His wife was a devout catholic so weekly mass at a minimum was a foregone conclusion. He had to laugh when he joined the local country club, something he swore he would never do. Next to his newfound family, his greatest joy came from his creation and management of his philanthropic charities. What amazed him was the more he gave, the more he received in return. All his businesses were so successful, new staff had to be hired on a continuing basis. It seems that once he got involved in community affairs, people appreciated his efforts and supported his many companies.

All these things made Vivian happy. She saw her son marry a wonderful woman and give her four beautiful grandchildren. He became an extremely successful businessman in their community and initiated many charitable enterprises. She had often dwelled on the past when she was a prisoner confined to a wheelchair, locked inside herself with no means of escape. She would then recall that incredibly happy day when the veil was lifted, and she became a functioning person once again, able to remember the faces around her and recognize the ones she loved. After all, that's what a mother wants, to love and be loved.

Everyone surrounding Rocco benefitted from his life-changing experience, especially Rocco. He would live for many years and see his children's children grow to adulthood. But he was ever grateful that his mother never again inquired as to what Sarah had meant by "your past life", and "something your mother can be proud of?"

Chapter 6

The days were long for Sarah. She was still a young girl and often felt fatigue overshadow the excitement of her unending encounters each day. So, each mid-morning and mid-afternoon she afforded herself the luxury of a fifteen-minute break to enjoy a cool beverage and have a brief chat with her mom. She looked forward to the refreshing pitcher of iced tea that awaited her each afternoon. It somehow was always present on the front porch and she didn't know the source. She had always been a lemonade girl but had recently found iced tea as an alternate beverage. Whoever supplied her daily treat brewed the tea, you could tell it was never made from instant powder. Fresh lemons and just the right amount of sugar enhanced the flavor. Even the ice was clear and made the drink that much more tasteful. The pitcher was always on a serving tray depicting some sort of an action hero which Sarah found quite amusing. She figured her benefactor was a young boy and wanted to meet him. She didn't have to wait very long.

Jack Wancsak was a classmate of Sarah's and lived a few blocks over from her street. He'd had a boyhood crush on Sarah ever since kindergarten but never expressed his feelings for her. So, he continued his one-sided relationship at a distance either out of embarrassment or fear of rejection. After watching Sarah courageously interact with the crowds of people seeking her help, he couldn't stay in the shadows any longer and had to make his move.

Jack was a kind and energetic person. He was the oldest of three boys and took on the responsibility of helping to run his family's household. Both of his parents worked full time outside of the home, so Jack was the main caregiver after school while the three boys waited for their parents to return from work. On most days he started dinner for his mom and did most of the yard work for his dad. He had a grass cutting business in the neighborhood to earn spending money. Jack took his responsibilities very seriously and maintained the lawns as well as any lawn service. He walked his route everyday checking each lawn. He was there to cut the grass and do the edging before any of his customers had to make a call. His business continued to grow by word of mouth. His customers loved him.

While making his way from house to house, dragging his equipment on a makeshift cart, Jack got to watch Sarah each day. It was on one of these trips through the neighborhood that Jack noticed the exhausted look on Sarah's face. He stopped and watched Sarah from behind a tree as she moved from person to person, healing and giving words of encouragement. Whether out of his secret love for Sarah or pure compassion, he knew he had to do something to alleviate her discomfort. Jack was an iced tea junkie and wanted to share this little quirk with his secret sweetheart. He devised a plan and each day he prepared the pitcher and had it placed on her front porch in time for her afternoon break. For the time being, he wanted to remain anonymous but one day he was behind schedule with his lawn care business and his cover was blown.

Recent heavy rains had caused an explosion of growth and he had to cut more lawns then usual each day to keep them under control. After the last yard was cut and edged, he loaded his equipment on the cart and made his way home. He had already brewed the tea so all that was left to do was combine the lemon, sugar and ice with the tea in a pitcher, grab a tray and a glass and head off to Sarah's. He made his way through the crowd and arrived at his destination. He took the steps up to the front porch two at a time and was stopped in his tracks at the top of the stairs. There sitting on the porch was Sarah and her mom. A look of surprise spread over Jack's and Sarah's face, as he came to a screeching halt. Jack snatched the pitcher in midair as it went flying from the tray, avoiding the loss of his precision cargo.

"You're busted," said Sarah. At that, all three of them laughed. Natalie, sensing an awkward moment for a parent to be involved, excused herself and went into her home leaving the two to rest and relax on the porch.

Jack excused his appearance. He had just come from maintaining the lawns for three of his customers and was covered with sweat and smelled like grass. Talking about his lawn business helped break the ice and soon the two were chatting away.

"I never expected that you were the iced tea phantom. I saw you in class every day, well at least while I was going to school. Why haven't you ever talked to me? We've been together since kindergarten and I'll bet you haven't said two words to me. I don't bite."

"Now that you caught me red-handed I guess I have to come clean. I've had a crush on you ever since I first saw you. I know it was stupid not to talk to you but hey, I'm a guy and that's the best excuse I can come up with."

Their repeated laughs helped to ease the jitters they both felt. They talked about their families, the latest music-and other things relevant to eleven-year-old kids. Jack expressed his love of sports and particularly baseball. But due to his responsibilities to his family and his customers, he explained he couldn't join the team at school.

Sarah listened with an attentive ear and enjoyed his company. After an awkward break in the conversation, Sarah glanced over and saw a puzzled look on Jack's face. Wanting him to be comfortable in her presence, she said, "Go ahead, Jack, ask me what's on your mind."

"What's it like, I mean how did this all happen to you? Do you like what you have become?"

"I haven't become anything, I'm still an eleven-year-old just like you. I just happen to have a special gift from God that allows me to help others by healing their ailments."

"I believe in God," Jack said, "but can't even imagine what all this stuff is like. How did it happen? Have you actually seen God?"

"Wow, that's a lot of questions to throw at me. I'll try and explain as best I can."

Sarah spend the better part of the remaining break time telling Jack the story of her ministry, all the while sipping the iced tea and watching his reaction. She felt good being in the company of someone her own age and just talking at their level. Eventually, she glanced at her watch and noticed how the precious time for her break had passed. She excused herself and asked if Jack would like to join her and her mom for dinner. He jumped at the chance. After gathering his pitcher, glass and tray, he started to head for the steps. Sarah grabbed his arm and turned him around to face her and said, "What's the deal with the super hero trays?"

An instant blush spread over his face. "These are the only trays I could find, I hope you don't mind."

"I think it's cute," and with that she did the most unexpected thing-she reached forward and kissed him on the cheek. His blush intensified to the point he thought his face would catch on fire. Nothing more was said.

He made his way home, not walking but skipping on cloud nine. He felt he had met the most beautiful girl in the world and was upset with himself for never talking to Sarah before today. After arriving home, he explained to his mom that he would not be there for dinner and literally floated up the stairs. He showered and picked out his best shirt and jeans to wear. Most of his clothes he had purchased with the money earned from his lawn business, so he was particularly proud of how well he looked on these special occasions. He got ready so quickly that he had considerable time to kill before returning to Sarah's. He sat in the living room staring at the clock on the wall. The time moved so slowly for Jack, he wanted so badly to be with Sarah again. But on the other hand, he didn't want to seem so anxious, so he decided to arrive about five minutes later than the agreed upon time. He heard that that was called being fashionably late.

Jack said good-byes to his family and made the trek back to Sarah's. When he arrived at the Martinelli's he was surprised to see Sarah still among the crowd of people, praying, touching, talking and smiling. He started to get irritated. This was supposed to be his time with Sarah. Why was she still out there? Tomorrow was a school day, so he would have to be home by nine to finish his homework and get to bed. It was already after six and these people were eating away at his time with Sarah. Not wanting to cause a scene, Jack walked up the steps to the porch and took the same seat he had occupied earlier in the day. He could only watch as Sarah cured the faithful, all the while wanting to have her all to himself. It was almost an hour before Sarah excused herself from the gathered masses and made her way from the street to her home. When she reached the top of the steps she saw the upset look on Jack's face and immediately felt bad for her delay. She had forgotten she had invited Jack to dinner due to the demands of the day and tried to apologize as best she could. She sensed Jack's disappointment and poured on her innocent charm which worked in an instant. Sarah found out she could make Jack blush at the drop of a hat and continued to use that in her arsenal of female tricks to get what she wanted from him, most of the time. They both laughed and went into the house to have their evening meal together with Sarah's mom.

A little after nine, Jack excused himself and left for his home. While walking, he revisited all that had happened that day. Now that he had gotten to know Sarah, he somehow knew he wanted to spend the rest of his life with her. He didn't consider their age, he only knew that Sarah was a remarkable girl. He felt so comfortable around her and loved how easy it was to talk and laugh with her. Lying in bed that night, he tossed and turned, sleep just wouldn't come for him. The thought of their next time together totally occupied his thoughts and he continued to mull over it. Finally, in the wee hours of the morning, Jack succumbed to sleep from pure mental exhaustion.

Chapter 7

Sarah and her mom straightened up the dining room and kitchen and retired to the living room for some much-needed down time together. Sitting in silence and observing her daughter, Natalie could see some subtle changes coming over Sarah. She recalled how giddy and spirited Sarah had acted during dinner. It must have been her interaction with someone of her own age that triggered these changes in behavior. She had always been a popular girl with plenty of friends. Sarah's house was always a welcome place to go and hang which made Natalie happy. She always wanted Sarah's friends to consider their home open to everyone and always a safe place to go. The other parents never hesitated in allowing their kids permission to go to the Martinelli home for the evening. They all knew Natalie was a mother with strict house rules when it came to proper behavior.

They sat for some time before Natalie finally broke the silence.

"I really like Jack, how about you?"

"What Mom, did you say something?"

"Yes, I did. I said isn't Jack a sweet boy?"

"Oh yes, he certainly is. I really have come to like him."

"Why hasn't he ever been here before? From what he said at dinner, he doesn't live that far from us."

"I asked him the same thing this afternoon. We have been in school together since kindergarten but somehow we just never connected."

There was a pause in the conversation then Sarah started again.

"It was nice today having him here for dinner. I'm around so much pain and suffering each day so it was great to be around someone my own age. I'm not complaining because look at the outcome of the work I do. But Mom, I'm still only eleven and have my whole life ahead of me."

"I know, dear, I think about your life and your happiness all the time. I often wonder how this is going to play out for you. Will you be afforded the opportunity to develop relationships? Will you find Mr. Right and have a family? These can all be distractions so how much effort will you have to pour into your ministry and how much time will you have left for your own life? I know you were happy to accept this task in answer to God's calling, but what can we expect for your personal life? Right now, we can't answer that."

"You're right, Mom, I can't answer that. Am I wrong to want those things in my life? We have been so blessed and I was so happy to be called by God. But now, after I have had contact with someone my own age, someone that you can see is special, I am starting to have my doubts. I'm so torn. When I am around Jack, I feel young again. Those little simple things in life take on a whole new meaning. When I'm doing God's will, I feel the weight of the world pressing me down. I feel guilty taking breaks just to eat and rest. I feel guilty if I'm not outside at the crack of dawn to help relieve the physical and mental suffering in the world. I feel guilty if I'm not out there until after dark. Do you know what it's like to tell the person next to you that you can't touch them and cure them right now and that they will have to come back in the morning because you're tired? To see the disappointed look on their face knowing they will have to leave and make their way back to me the next day? But I can't go on twenty-four hours a day. I need my time, too. Is that being selfish? Was I the right one that should have been chosen for this ministry? Help me sort this all out, Mom. Maybe someone else would have been better than me."

Natalie could see the same evil at work that had previously affected her. She had prayed for relief of the doubts and anxiety and had found her peace. Apparently, it was all catching up to Sarah now. After all she was only eleven and perhaps the burden of her work was too much for someone so young. She would have to take Sarah into her confidence and let her know how she fell into a state of apprehension and doubt and how she received the strength she needed from God to support her daughter.

Natalie confided in Sarah, something she thought she would never do. She always believed parents were supposed to be strong in front of their kids, weren't they? There would be no easy solution to Sarah's dilemma tonight. Natalie told Sarah to pray to God for guidance just as she had done. Natalie felt confident Sarah's prayers would be answered.

It was getting late, so they decided to retire. Sarah took her shower and dressed for bed. When she was under the covers, Natalie came into her room to kiss her goodnight. She once again tried to reassure Sarah that things would work out if she prayed to God for help. Natalie tucked the covers up and around Sarah so tightly that she took on the appearance of an Egyptian mummy. They both laughed. Natalie switched off the light, and left closing the door behind her. No sooner had her mother left then Sarah heard her name called out. At first, she thought it was her mother then realized it was a masculine sounding voice. She reached over and switched on the table lamp. There, standing next to the bed, was Jesus. Sarah gasped in surprise.

"Hello, Sarah. I came to check on you."

"You couldn't have come at a better time. Jesus, I'm so confused. I'm trying to follow what you told me, but other things keep getting in the way and distracting me. Like today, I met a boy from my neighborhood and it made me stop and think about all that I'm missing in my life. Is this right to do? Shouldn't I be happy doing what you asked of me knowing how much I'm helping people and especially helping to lead them back to you? Why is this happening to me? Why can't I be stronger and put these doubts and desires behind me?"

Jesus sat on the edge of the bed before He addressed her concerns. As He sat, Sarah looked up into his eyes. Instantly, she found a warmth and comfort that she hadn't noticed before. During their last encounter, Sarah perceived physical warmth when they embraced. But this transcended anything physical, it was spiritual in nature. At that instant, Sarah remembered a passage in scripture. It pertained to one of the times after the resurrection of Christ when He appeared to his disciples. While standing in their midst He repeated three times, "Peace be to you." Jesus was aware of the fear in their hearts over concern for their own safety. His disciples feared that they would be the next to suffer because of their relationship with Him. It took these simple words to quell their fears. He further assured them of the coming of the Spirit and at once all their concerns were put to rest. How did this passage suddenly come into her consciousness? She saw a slight smile appear on Jesus' face and a wonderful twinkle in his eyes.

"Jesus, you are amazing," was all she could muster. "You knew exactly what I needed and when I needed it. Thank you".

"Oh, dear Sarah, you never cease to surprise me. You are like a clean canvas waiting for the artist. You accept everything in its time and produce such wonders. I couldn't be any prouder of one of my creations. You have never let me down and are following my instructions to the letter. Please find peace in your heart. You have touched the lives of so many already and given them such hope.

"I understand that you are pulled between two worlds, the one of youth and the other of disciple and evangelist. I know this is not an easy task, but I chose you because I believe in you. I know the strength that lies beneath that youthful exterior and have seen you performing your mission with great enthusiasm and joy. The shortcomings you feel like doubt and guilt are natural and I don't want you to worry. You will lead a normal life, find the right man to call your husband and bear children of your own. You are already sacrificing so much for me I couldn't allow your life to be altered in such a drastic way as to prevent your happiness. Again, I say, peace be to you."

Sarah reached up and embraced Jesus. She did find the peace she sought.

"This was a needed visit because I have to talk with you about your mission and the changes we have to make. So far, we have been conducting your ministry in your area. Many people from around the world have traveled here as you know, but we need to be true evangelists and travel to other peoples. Many don't have the resources to make the pilgrimage to you, so you must go to them. Early in your ministry I had many saints and martyrs visit with you. I wanted them to explain in their own words what it was like for them to journey to foreign lands and to spread the good news. Now you understand why it was so important for you to meet with them and get their impressions first hand."

"I remember every encounter and loved each one. So, I guess I'm supposed to be a modern-day St. Paul and go to the Romans and Ephesians and Corinthians and Colossians?"

"Something like that. So, in preparation for your journey I am giving you your next gift, the gift of tongues. You will be able to understand everyone that approaches you and speak with them, no matter what their language or dialect. This gift is necessary for you to put the faithful at ease when they approach you and are healed. They need to believe in me and long for eternal salvation. Do you understand what this gift means to you?"

"Yes, I do." The excitement was quite evident in Sarah's voice. "This is going to be an amazing experience. Where are we going? Mom and I have never been able to travel because we just didn't have the money. I always wanted to see other lands and other peoples; this is going to be great."

"Soon, very soon. But Bishop Wallace has the sports arena in town scheduled for your use over the next few weeks. I know this is going to be more difficult for you, it was so easy for you to leave your home and minister here in your neighborhood. But the local roads are becoming over-taxed with all the faithful journeying to you, so we must move to a location that affords greater access. Bishop Wallace has been very energetic in his sponsoring and promoting your ministry, so I don't want to disappoint him and move you to a foreign location just yet. I don't want to bruise his delicate ego now that he has reformed his life."

Sarah smiled at Jesus' remarks after remembering Bishop Wallace's conversion at her hands. And she agreed that they should make use of the sports arena which would allow for adequate time to plan the trip overseas."

"Dear Jesus, thank you for making this visit to me. I really needed your help and was prepared to pray very hard tonight, but you anticipated my needs and arrived just in time to help me through this tough period." Sarah hesitated before garnering the nerve to ask her next question.

"Jesus, what can you tell me about Jack? Is he the one for me? I really like him and think he likes me."

Jesus paused before he spoke to prepare his remarks in such a way that would be relevant to a girl of eleven years. "The dating and courting process is very complicated, one of the most complicated in human behavior. This is due mostly to the differences between males and females and the wants and needs of each. A young lady wants to be swept off her feet by a brave and strong man, have the door held open for her, receive flowers and be told how great she looks when she wears an outfit for the first time. The young guy wants someone he can be proud of when he walks down the street. He wants everyone's eyes to turn and see him and the girl he has on his arm. He wants someone who is loving and nurturing, can keep a nice looking home and knows her way around the kitchen. These are the qualities she will need to raise a family, which is the ultimate purpose of the marriage union, to continue the species with their genetic makeup. During the dating period, individuals will find happiness and sadness, thrills and disappointments, satisfaction and let downs, fulfillment and emptiness. It is a very complex period of one's life and I would never want to spare you of all the emotional highs and lows associated with it. If I told you Jack or another person was the one for you, the thrill of waiting for your guy to arrive to take you on a date would not be realized. The first kiss, the holding of the hands would be less meaningful. The emotional high and the flood of hormones when you've found the right man would have less of an impact. I want you to lead a normal life and I want you to experience all that goes with being a young woman. Exploring and acting on all these facets of your personal life are up to you. Knowing the type of girl you are and the woman you will become, I feel confident it will be an enriching period in your life. One in which I will not interfere."

After carefully listening to Jesus' words, Sarah found great happiness and gratitude that she would be able to pursue a personal life of her own even though her ministry would occupy most of her time. She held this meeting with Jesus close to her heart and frequently thought of his words and what could be expected on her personal journey. Through this encounter with Jesus, Sarah obtained the peace of mind she needed. The evil forces that had attempted to corrupt her and lead her into doubt and depression had been conquered and eliminated and would no longer be an effective distraction. Sarah and Jesus had a final embrace, and in an instant, He vanished from her sight. That night, Sarah experienced a restful sleep like none before.

During their breakfast together the next morning, Sarah informed her mom of the changes that would have to take place immediately to utilize the sports arena. Natalie decided it would be best to initiate a call to Bishop Wallace to work out all the details. After their early morning meal, Sarah kissed her mom good-bye and made her way to the faithful. Natalie placed the call to Bishop Wallace.

The Bishop brought Natalie up to speed on the arrangements at the arena and that he had coordinated limousine service to be at their disposal each day from the many companies offering the limos at no cost. He further informed her that he had received multiple offers from hotels and private homes in the immediate area of the arena for her and Sarah to stay if they would so choose. Natalie thought it best if they return to their home each day and keep some type of normalcy to their hectic lives. Bishop Wallace offered no objection.

So, for the next few weeks, Sarah and Natalie were driven to and from the sports arena each day in style, a departure from the rusted out old clunker they usually drove. It took a couple of days for Sarah to feel comfortable in the new surroundings but eventually she adapted well to the change.

Often, during her down time when she wasn't administering to those that sought her aid she would think about her upcoming trip to Europe. She would inquire daily concerning the progress that had been made and how the itinerary was developing. She had to know which cities they would be visiting, how long they would be there, what activities had been planned by the locals and what type of venue she would occupy while conducting her ministry. Natalie finally had to put a halt to Sarah's constant inquires and told her she would find everything out when it was time to leave and that she should fully concentrate on her interaction with the faithful. Sarah agreed to the restraints and asked her mom for forgiveness. Natalie assured her there was nothing to forgive and that she understood how she could be so excited of the upcoming trip.

The frequency with which Sarah and Jack visited with each other dramatically diminished. At first, Jack would wait on the front porch for Sarah to return home in the evening. But she was often delayed, and Jack had to worry about caring for his siblings, finishing his homework and maintaining the lawns for his customers. So, after many disappointing nights Jack decided to call Sarah by phone instead of waiting on the porch. But that arrangement got strained because of Sarah's inconsistent schedule. Finally, Jack stopped calling Sarah, the frustration just got to be too much for him to bear.

It was time for Sarah to make her first European mission, but she didn't want to leave Jack on such terms. The night before she was scheduled to leave, she made the call. Jack answered on the third ring.

"Hello."

"Hello Jack, this is Sarah. I haven't heard from you for a while." She paused before continuing.

"I understand how you can be so upset and why you have been avoiding me. I told you from the start that I had to be focused on what I was doing and couldn't let anything distract me from what I was told to do by God. If I hurt you, I'm sorry. I would never want to hurt anyone especially you."

"It has been tough not seeing you all the time like I used to. I liked being with you and thought you liked being with me."

"That's not the point. Of course, I liked being with you, but we had to move downtown to the sports arena and that really made it tough on me and my mom. But we had to do it. And now I have some more bad news for you. Tomorrow, me and my mom leave for Europe, Rome to be exact. Staying here isn't easy for everyone else so we need to go to them. Rome is just the first of many cities that we are scheduled to visit. And after that, I don't know. We may be going to Africa or Asia."

Jack was devastated. All his dreams of spending time with his girl were blown away in an instant. He loved being in her company and most of all he loved their conversations. Now there would be a major void in his life, one that could not be easily filled.

After a few parting words, Jack ended the call. Sarah could sense the disappointment in his voice and knew she had hurt her friend. But things were in motion in every aspect of her life and there was no altering the schedule. Not knowing when they would return, Sarah couldn't leave Jack under these conditions. She pleaded with her mom and got permission to go and visit Jack with the condition that Natalie would accompany her to the Wancsak house. They made the short walk and soon were knocking on Jack's front door.

Jack's mom answered the door and was surprised to see Sarah and her mom on their front steps. After pleasantries were exchanged, Jack was called down from his room and he and Sarah took a walk while Natalie spent time with Jack's mom. After they got into a steady walking pace, Jack reached down and took Sarah's hand. She loved the feeling and bumped his shoulder with hers. He reciprocated with a gentle smile.

"Sarah, I don't know what to tell you. I think about you all the time, when I'm in school and at home and cutting my lawns. We just have gotten to know each other but I feel like you've been in my life forever and that's the way I want it to be. Now you're leaving, what am I supposed to do?" Then kidding he said, "Who am I going to make iced tea for?"

That helped to ease the tension they both felt.

"I pray every day for guidance," said Sarah. "I really care for you and love having you in my life. When I'm around you, I forget about the stress in my life; I feel young again. I think that is kind of a gift from God. He knows that I need to be mature in my ministry when dealing with the faithful. But when you and I are together, all that goes away and I'm eleven again. I look forward to our time together and think God is pleased to give me that balance in my life. I'm leaving tomorrow but I don't want to lose contact with you. If this is something that we both want, we can make it work. What do you think?"

"I could never say good-bye to you. Of course, I want to stay in your life. Just tell me what to do and how to make this work and I'll do it."

"That's what I wanted to hear." They stopped walking and embraced. At that moment they both felt a serene calmness engulf them. They both sensed it and knew it was of a spiritual nature; it was like nothing they had ever felt before. They looked into each other's eyes and exchanged a glance of understanding.

They knew everything would be okay and would work out for them.

Sarah started to feel a chill and decided it was time to go. They made their way back to Jack's house in silence. Before leaving, Sarah and Jack worked out a schedule that Sarah would initiate a phone call every Sunday evening from where ever she was in Europe. Considering the time difference, Jack said he would make himself available to take the call every Sunday afternoon. With few additional words, they hugged, and Sarah and Natalie made their way home.

Chapter 8

Early the next morning, a limo arrived to whisk them away to their waiting private jet. Natalie made arrangements with her close friends and neighbors to care for their home while they were away. Everyone was glad to pitch in for so many had been helped by Sarah's healing touch.

Sarah marveled at the flight experience. She had never been on a plane before let alone a private, luxury jet. It was difficult to peel her away from her window, even during the long ride across the Atlantic Ocean. She continued to stare out at the beauty of God's creation from 35,000 feet. She issued a constant volley of questions to her flight crew about their intended route, their current location, what landmarks she should be looking for, how high they were flying, the dynamics of the aircraft in flight, etc. This continued until Natalie suggested she rest for a while. One of the flight attendants placed a comfy pillow under her head and covered her with a fluffy, soft blanket. She then tilted her seat into a reclining position and dimmed the cabin lights. It wasn't long before Sarah drifted off for a much-needed nap.

As they once again were over land, Natalie woke Sarah as she had promised and instantly the questions made to the flight crew started. The jet's capacity was large enough that it didn't require refueling and they soon found themselves landing at the Leonardo da Vinci airport in Rome, Italy, late in the evening.

All the arrangements for their arrival were made and choreographed like a fine dance routine. Customs and immigration staff met them at the jet and went through the formalities of admission to their county and Europe. Each officer who had an encounter with Sarah was healed of their physical and mental ailments and expressed their appreciation and wished them God's blessing. After their exit, a limo arrived to transport them to their hotel suite in the heart of Rome. During the ride, Sarah asked her mom about their itinerary for the next couple of days. Sarah was happy to hear that the next day was set aside for a visit with the Pope and a tour of Vatican City. Through her overseas contacts Natalie was made aware of the Pope's desire to meet with Sarah and was only too happy to fulfill his request. Sarah was also made aware that she would conduct her ministry from St. Peter's Square in the shadow of St. Peter's Basilica. She agreed with all the arrangements and couldn't wait to start her European mission. Natalie calmed her down and they made their way through the avenues and streets of Rome mostly in silence. It was dark, but Sarah couldn't resist straining to see what she could as they made their way to their destination.

They arrived at their hotel to find a small crowd assembled. Word had gotten out about Sarah's trip to Rome and many faithful wanted to experience her healing powers immediately. Sarah was only too happy to oblige and for the next two hours, walked among the Romans just as St. Paul had done two thousand years earlier.

When the crowd had weaned to a trickle, Sarah knew it was time to retire and entered the hotel with Natalie where they were escorted to their room. It was a luxurious suite of rooms that had multiple balconies overlooking the city. Sarah just stood on the balcony outside of her room and stared for the longest time. She couldn't believe all that was happening to her and at such an early age. She thanked God for all his wonderful gifts and silently prayed for guidance and assurance that she was conducting her ministry as He wanted.

After a while, Natalie made her come in and prepare for bed. Tomorrow like so many days before would be long and tiring. But before she would go to bed, Sarah had to call Jack and tell him of today's incredible journey and all that she had seen. They stayed on the phone talking so long that Sarah started to doze. Unable to complete a sentence without losing Sarah, Jack thought it best to end the call and let his special girl get some sleep. They said their good-byes and agreed to talk the following Sunday. Sarah retired with the doors to her balcony open. She instantly fell into a deep sleep to the cadence of the sounds of Rome echoing in her mind.

The sun spread its rays across the balcony and floor of Sarah's room and this brought her back to consciousness. She wanted to experience everything possible and didn't want to waste any more time in bed then was absolutely needed. She got out of bed and left her room to find her mom already up and sitting on her balcony sipping a cup of espresso. Breakfast had been delivered to their suite a few minutes earlier, so they made their way to the dining area and began their morning meal. They both ate more than they usually would have. They both commented on how foods always taste better when prepared by someone else. Sarah ate so fast that her mom had to slow her down. Her excuse was she wanted to hurry and get ready to make her trip to visit with the Pope and start her tour. Natalie understood her excitement and excused her from the table. A short time later they were showered and changed into the beautiful outfits that had been delivered to their room. Natalie was surprised that even their sizes of clothing and footwear were known by their generous benefactors. But she had learned long ago not to question things of this nature. It all had a way of working itself out.

They left their suite and made their way to the hotel lobby. Along the way, countless individuals approached Sarah and begged for her healing powers. She naturally complied and after a short delay, they made their way down the circular ramp that led from the hotel to their limo. The morning drive through Rome was exhilarating for them. As they headed west, they peered from the back of the limo up at the ancient monuments, astonished at both their beauty and ruggedness. How could these structures stand the test of time? What architectural geniuses created such wonders?

They made their way over the Tiber River and around the Piazza Adriana. Next it was down the Via Della Conciliazione and around the Piazza San Pietro until they came within sight of the most breathtaking view of all, that of Basilica di San Pietro, St. Peter's Basilica. The size and majesty of the buildings and surrounding gardens took their breath away. Sarah just couldn't believe that such beauty could exist that was created by man. But then she paused to reflect that these creations were inspired by God and put into the hearts of men and women.

The limo took a little-known route to a private entrance normally reserved for dignitaries and heads of state. They were instantly greeted by an emissary of the Pontiff and escorted through the hallowed halls of the Vatican to the Pope's private chapel. Along the way they passed Swiss Guards that were stationed at entry ways and along corridors. Sarah smiled at the first few but when they didn't reciprocate, she knew they were required to remain motionless and soon gave up trying to get them to react to her kind gesture. Pope John Paul III was already in the chapel waiting for his guests. He was an energetic man of sixty-eight whose appearance belied his true age. But recently he had been diagnosed with Parkinson's disease and the initial symptoms were becoming apparent as each day passed. He attempted to hide this from the public, but the signs of the disease were becoming more apparent and soon the world would know.

The Pontiff greeted Natalie and Sarah, and each bowed to kiss his ring. Before she initiated her bow, Sarah prayed for the pope and asked God to heal any of his ailments; she could not have known of any of his existing conditions. As she bowed to kiss his ring she grasped his hand and continued to pray. Instantly, the healing graces of God spread through the Pontiff's body and all signs of the disease were eradicated. He felt the change coming over him and gasped in astonishment. He reached down and placed his hands on both of Sarah's shoulders. He looked into her eyes and said, "How did you know?"

"I didn't until we made contact. I always place my trust in the hands of the Lord. He has never let me or anyone else down."

The pontiff said a simple thank you which was all that was needed. He was about to say his daily mass and asked if they would like to join him. They were overwhelmed at the privilege and relocated to the nearest pew in front of the altar. At communion time, they approached the altar and received the Blessed Sacrament under both species, first the sacred host and then the sacred blood from the Pope's chalice. Sarah had never felt so close to God as she did at that moment. She felt it was an experience that even rivaled her visits with Jesus. Natalie and Sarah returned to their pew, lowered their heads and thanked God for all their blessings.

When mass was over, the Pope excused himself, so he could remove his vestments. He had them escorted to an anteroom where they could wait for his return. He joined them for a while on their tour and had to excuse himself when they entered the Sistine Chapel. He had a full schedule that day and promised to meet with them again later.

Their guide was thoroughly knowledgeable about the history of the chapel. He went on to explain that the ceiling frescos were by Michelangelo and that they dominated the room. The side wall tapestries were by Raphael and depicted events from the Gospels and the Acts of the Apostles. Other wall paintings were divided or partitioned into the concept of world history; the time before the Ten Commandments were given to Moses, between Moses and the birth of Christ, and the Christian era. They spent a considerable amount of time in the chapel then left to resume their tour.

Much of the papal quarters that weren't off limits were visited next and eventually they made their way to the cavernous abyss of the basilica. They strained their necks and eyes to follow the lead of their guide as he pointed out all the nuances of the majestic building. They ended their tour by entering the crypt where many of the popes were laid to rest. Sarah had been visited by a number of these saints and smiled to herself each time she passed one of the names that she recognized.

When their tour was completed they were escorted back to the papal quarters to have a final meeting with the Pope. They met in his dining area where they snacked on petite Italian pastries and espresso and engaged in light conversation. It was growing late and they each agreed to call it a day. Sarah and Natalie knew that tomorrow would be one of the most demanding days. The story of their journeying to Rome was well publicized and record numbers were expected in St. Peter's Square. Before leaving his holiness, Natalie and Sarah received a papal blessing. Pope John Paul III said he was only reciprocating the blessing that Sarah had given him through Our Lord. They all laughed at his levity. They left after giving a promise to visit with him before they left Rome.

On their way to their hotel it was decided that they would have dinner in their room which would allow them the maximum amount of restful time together. Any attempt to walk the streets and dine at a local bistro would cause too much disruption.

Once in their suite they changed into comfy clothes and moved to the balcony off Natalie's room where they dined. The sun was setting and cast long-fingered shadows over the landscape. A crimson hue blended with a rich pallet of colors to paint the sky in an unimaginable scene of beauty and awe. Seated in adjoining chairs they held hands and surveyed the magnificence of their surroundings mostly in silence. Eventually, the evening chill and fatigue overtook them, and they retired for the day. Still feeling the effects of jetlag coupled with their exhaustive schedule left Sarah so tired that she couldn't remember hitting her pillow. She slipped into such a deep sleep that when she arose in the morning she was totally refreshed and without any memory of her overnight dreams. Before rising from her bed, she said her morning prayers and thanked God for the restful night and begged for the strength to fulfill her mission according to his wishes.

The first week in Rome came and went with Sarah following pretty much the same schedule each day. But on the tenth day she had an encounter with a remarkable woman. The previous few days Sarah had noticed a woman observing her, but the woman seemed too timid to approach her. She always stood a few paces away but never came to her for her curing. The woman was of classic Italian beauty. Tall and lean with striking eyes so dark they almost looked black. Her jet-black hair was perfectly sculpted and embraced her oval face. She always dressed in incredible fashion that hugged her shapely body. When she walked she did so with authority even though she balanced on four-inch heels. Sarah was moved by the Spirit to approach her and took the initiative to do so. Sarah moved in her direction healing the faithful as she progressed. Each time she moved closer the women moved away. After about the fifth occurrence the woman was backed against a group of people that couldn't be moved because of the cramped surroundings. She just stood there as Sarah approached closer and closer. Finally, next to her Sarah said, "Buon giorno."

"Buon giorno, bella ragazza," was the woman's reply. They continued in Italian.

"I've noticed you for the past few days, but you never come to me to be healed. You shouldn't be afraid to receive this wonderful gift from God. Can I touch you now? I promise you it will heal you of all of your physical and mental ailments."

"I'm not here for a physical healing, little one. I have destroyed my life and don't deserve to be healed like all of these here next to me."

"Then why do you come here day after day? Now that I am close to you I can see the pain and suffering in your eyes. Why wouldn't you want to feel God's healing graces?"

"Because I don't deserve it."

"Then why are you here?"

"I'm here to beg for God's forgiveness. If you are so close to God, you must speak to him on my behalf. I want you to intercede for me and have him forgive my lifetime of sin."

"What is your name?"

"I've been called so many things, whore, prostitute, lady of the night. They all mean the same. But my given name is Regina. Do you know what that means?"

"It means queen."

"Yes, and I have been the queen of the whores."

"Do you want to tell me why you are so bitter and why you can't give in to God's healing graces?"

"I guess I should tell you if you are to seek my forgiveness."

Sarah approached her and reached out to take her hand. Regina pulled back not wanting to feel Sarah's touch. But Sarah assured her she would not pray for her healing, she just wanted to be close to her and ease her nervousness. Regina complied and took Sarah's hand into hers. She looked down at the loving and compassionate face before her and began to weep. Sarah squeezed her hand and spoke comforting words to her which calmed her immediately. Regina began telling her story.

"I have always been a beautiful woman. Men have always sought me out, mostly as a trophy to rest on their arm, you know, something to brag about. I wanted to be a world class supermodel and actress and had the looks to make it. But partying and booze and drugs seemed to be more important and I got to the point where I couldn't get modeling jobs any longer. I had to earn money, so I could eat so I turned to the only other thing that I could do, and that was to make men happy. Because of my looks I could demand the highest price for an evening of pleasure. For years I had a distinctive clientele that paid top dollar for my services. But then I got careless and greedy. I wanted to put this whole mess behind me and retire by using all that I had saved over the years. To rush to this early retirement, I started accepting clients that, shall I say, were less desirable. And on one of these occasions I contracted the HIV. As soon as I knew of the disease in my system I stopped working. Eventually it turned to full blown AIDS and now I'm dying a slow death." She had to pause to collect herself and wipe the tears from her eyes.

"I had everything, the looks and the brains to go with them. But the pleasures of the body took central focus in my life and I blew all the opportunities I had. The partying with high rollers and the movers and shakers along with the drugs became too irresistible. Too often I was hung over and couldn't keep up with the demanding schedule I had gotten myself into with my career.

I either arrived late and couldn't perform before the camera or I didn't make the appointments at all. A few of these slipups and I was blackballed from the industry. Time is money and money is all that matters. It took me a while to clean up and get the drugs out of my life. During that time, I accepted money from any man who wanted me. But soon I started to be more selective and kept my sights on the big money clients. I used my looks and skills to my advantage and for years that was the perfect formula for success. But as I said, I wanted out of this maze and started to accept clients I wouldn't normally take as customers. That was my downfall and the beginning of my end.

"I have led a deplorable life. One of which I am not proud and would never wish on anyone. It was great while it lasted but now I must pay the price for my recklessness and stupidity. I don't deserve to be cured; all I am asking for is forgiveness from God. It's hard to know how much time remains. The doctors say only months. I don't want to die like this. Now in this stage of my life I have become more focused on God. I have destroyed my life, but I don't want to destroy my soul." She began to weep bitterly.

"Regina, during my ministry I have touched and cured thousands of the faithful and on occasion I have seen a glimpse of the sins in their lives. These have been powerful individuals, some of whom you would never expect to have a checkered past. They are no better or worse than you and the countless thousands that have come to me for God's mercy. Our souls are immortal, and it has always been God's plan to share eternal life with his creation. He wants each of us to share that life in Him and not be damned to a tortuous existence. We are all weak and on occasion commit sin which separates us from the connection with God. But God is forever forgiving and wants us back. No matter what the sin, if we are truly sorry He will take us back. It is a promise He has never broken. I am here out of His great mercy. My work is a sign to the world that God loves us and wants us to correct the mistakes in our lives. We must seek His love and forgiveness above all else and care for each other. These are His commands which can't be taken lightly. I believe you are truly sorry for the mistakes you have made in your life and you should allow me to pray for you and your immortal soul. We all get a second chance; it's knowing when to use it that counts. Don't be afraid any longer."

"You're right Sarah, I am afraid. I'm afraid God can't forgive me after I squandered all that I had in my life. But I am dying and need to come to God for forgiveness if I am ever to find peace in these last days. So, intervene for me and ask God to forgive me, that's all I ask."

Regina knelt to be at eye level with Sarah. She moved forward and kissed her on the cheek and thanked her for listening to her story. She said, "No matter what happens, thank you, beautiful girl." And with that, she closed her eyes and lowered her head.

Sarah released the hold on Regina's hand and placed both of her hands on the top of Regina's head. She closed her eyes and prayed to God for the forgiveness that this penitent woman sought. Instantly, the spirit of Sarah and Regina were transformed before Jesus. It was the same surroundings in which Sarah had witnessed her previous encounter with Jesus. Both of Jesus' hands were outstretched to receive theirs. They complied and Regina felt a calming peace. All her fears and anxiety were swept away, and she was at peace. She attempted to speak but was quieted by Jesus. He spoke first.

"Regina, my sister, your faith has saved you. I can see the sincerity in your heart and know that you are truly sorry for all the indiscretions in your life. The Father wants us all to be with Him for all eternity and you have done what needs to be done to secure your happiness in Him. Now come unto Him".

With those closing words the spirit of Regina vanished from their midst. Sarah stared at Jesus with the most puzzling look. Before she could inquire about what had just happened, Jesus spoke.

"It was her time. The Father has seen her suffering and has taken her home. She was sorry for misusing her life and has found that which she sought, forgiveness. Don't be saddened by the loss of her mortal life but rejoice in the salvation of her eternal soul."

"She was such a beautiful woman that had it all. When she came to me for help I couldn't refuse her request. But I never thought that my intersession would lead to her death. Please help me to understand."

"Regina was far more ill then you could visibly see. The AIDS virus was in its advanced stages and she was suffering. She didn't want to end her life by suicide for fear of the everlasting consequences. So, she remained true to the course of obtaining forgiveness before her death. Out of love and compassion she was called home."

"Why didn't she receive the healing power when I touched her? I know it wasn't what she wanted."

"You're right, it wasn't what she wanted. Your gift needs to be desired for it to take effect in the life of an individual. Regina wanted forgiveness and release from the strangle hold of her disease. She was granted that wish after she was found truly penitent for a lifetime of sin. She has obtained that which we all desire, eternal life; a life that will last forever with God."

"I understand but am saddened knowing what she must have had to endure. I will continue to pray for her."

"You do not have to pray for her but rather to her now that she is with the Father. You can pray to her for your own intercessions."

"Thank you, Jesus. This has been a truly remarkable and fulfilling experience and I am grateful".

"You are welcome. Now you must return to your mission, there are a few hundred thousand of the faithful waiting for you."

Sarah returned to her earthly consciousness. As she did, she noticed she still had her hands on the top of Regina's head. As she removed her hands, the physical body of Regina collapsed to the ground. As Sarah had expected, she was dead. The faithful in the immediate area gasped in disbelief. How could this happen? This was supposed to be a time of healing not of death. Sarah addressed them as follows, "She was called home to our heavenly Father; it was her time."

With that said, Sarah turned and encountered the next person seeking her help. Nearby first aid medics arrived at the site and placed Regina's body on a stretcher that they brought with them. They placed a cover over her remains and carried her away. Over the next few days, no one came to claim her body, so the authorities couldn't identify her. She was laid to rest in an unmarked grave.

Chapter 9

Sarah remained in Rome with Natalie for another month. But soon it was time to say arrivederci, Roma. They met with the Pope once more and he wished them well and gave them his papal blessing.

They journeyed to other major European cities to continue their mission; Paris, Barcelona, Berlin and Amsterdam to mention a few. Each stop lasted between four to six weeks. It was turning late fall so all concerned thought it best if they relocate to a warmer climate for the next few months so not to cause a hardship for Sarah. Australia was the next country to be visited.

They arrived in Sydney and remained there for almost eight weeks. When they had completed their allotted time, they headed south to Canberra then on to Melbourne. Next, they swung to the north and made their way to Brisbane and Cairns, stopping in as many towns along the way. Darwin was next and finally Perth.

Each Sunday, as promised, Sarah would make the phone call to Jack. She felt it important to keep in touch with her friend and maintain their long-distance relationship. No matter where she was at the time, it was the one thing on which she never wavered. Jack looked forward to the call and spent most of his day waiting by or near the phone. With Sarah's schedule and the time difference, he never could tell when the call would arrive. He never complained about the arrangement because he really cared for Sarah. Somewhere deep in his heart he knew their relationship would stand the test of time and someday they would be together.

Other than early mass, Jack set aside his Sundays in anticipation of Sarah's call. He worked late evenings during the week and most of Saturdays to keep his lawn service running. To occupy his time each Sunday he finished his homework, worked on the invoicing for his business, watched a little TV and read. He was becoming quite proficient in bookkeeping and accounting practices which would help in the future with his expanding lawn care business.

Sarah made the weekly call to Jack on what was to be the last Sunday in Perth. She waited as late as she could because of the fourteen-hour time difference. As soon as the phone rang Jack was on it and picked up the handset on the second ring.

"Hello."

"Hello Jack, its Sarah. How are you?"

"Much better now that you've called. How are you?"

"Tired. It's been a long and demanding day. This was our last day here and we'll be leaving the first thing in the morning. I remained with the faithful as long as I could. I know I'll be leaving a lot of disappointed souls behind but I'm sure I'll be back here in the future."

"Please tell me you're coming home."

There was a long pause. Sarah finally gave Jack the news he didn't want to hear.

"I'm sorry, Jack, but I'll be heading to Japan in the morning. We all agreed that our next stop should be to a nation that is not traditionally Christian so Japan was chosen because of its proximity to Australia. The weather is changing now so it made the most sense to go there next."

"I was hoping you would be coming home. You've been gone so long, and I really miss you."

"I miss you, too, but we've talked about this so many times. This is what I'm supposed to be doing right now in my life and everything else must be put on hold. I have no idea when I'll be back home to see you. I have to follow this mission no matter where it leads me, you have to understand that."

"I do, but it's really tough. I keep occupied with school work and my lawn service but at night when I'm in bed and have time to think you are always on my mind and I wish you were here."

"The separation has been tough on both of us but the thing I miss the most is your iced tea."

They both laughed at that and it seemed to lighten the mood a little.

Natalie was in the next room and couldn't help overhearing the conversation. She was touched by the innocence of their conversation and knew how much they cared for each other. A plan started to develop that she believed would temporarily ease their loneliness. It was important for Sarah to have friends her own age involved in her life. She was still eleven and at times Natalie wanted her daughter to be eleven and enjoy this period in her life. The responsibilities of the ministry weighed down on her, but she deserved a break from time to time and Natalie knew just what had to happen.

After they arrived in Tokyo, Natalie made the necessary calls to put her plan in motion. The last call she would have to make was to Jack's mom, Carol. They had met prior to leaving for Rome and Natalie appreciated the support and kindness she had shown Sarah.

"Hello, this is Carol. Who is calling please?"

"Hi Carol, its Natalie Martinelli. How are you?"

"Just fine. This is a surprise. Jack usually waits for Sarah's call on Sundays. I know they just talked yesterday so why the call today? It has to be late there and besides, Jack is in school now."

"I really wanted to talk to you, Carol. What would you say to you and Jack joining us for a couple of days in Tokyo? I have all the arrangements set for next week. I hate to spring this on you. I'm not sure if you can get off work on such short notice either but I think this is just what the doctor ordered for them. What do you say?"

"Wow, Natalie, that's a very generous offer. Did you mention any of this to Sarah?"

"No, not yet. I wanted to run it by you first. As a matter of fact, if you do decide to come, I'm not going to tell her. Her birthday is in a couple of weeks and I wanted to surprise her a little early. She never would expect this."

I'll talk with my husband tonight and if we can get my mom to watch the other two boys, we'll be happy to make the trip. I think I can answer for Jack with a great big YES."

"Great. I'll call you the same time tomorrow with all the details. It was nice talking with you."

"Same here. I'll talk to you tomorrow."

That evening, Jack was bouncing off the walls when he heard the news. Carol and her husband came to the same conclusion that it would be great for Jack to see Sarah, even for a few days. Natalie called the next day as promised and gave Carol the schedule. The timetable was agreeable, and Natalie closed with wishing them a safe trip.

The week seemed to drag for Jack, particularly in school. He got his teachers to give him the assignments that were to be completed during the trip and Jack had them all done before they left for Japan. He made sure all his lawns were cut and trimmed so he could go with a clear conscience. Saturday finally came, and it was time to leave.

A limo arrived at their home and shuttled them to a private airstrip not too far from their home. Carol and Jack made their way from the limo to the jet and boarded it after turning over their bags to their flight attendant. Within minutes they were on their way. Refueling stops were made on the west coast and Hawaii and after almost twenty-four hours, they set down at the Narita International Airport in Tokyo. Jack slept very little during his journey out of sheer excitement. He felt fortunate to be making the trip. How many kids get a chance to experience anything like this? he thought. But more importantly, he was going to see his Sarah.

It was late Sunday evening in Tokyo. Sarah knew she would soon be talking to Jack and every time she thought about the upcoming Sunday evening call she felt goose bumps up and down her spine. It was common practice that one of Sarah's local assistants would place the call. Having to go through the local phone companies and the use of international calling numbers would have made it tough for a non-local to place a call. Sarah was handed the handset after the call was placed. She heard the phone ring four times before it was answered.

"Hello Sarah, this is Jack."

"Hi Jack." Then Sarah commented, "This connection is so clear it's like you're in the next room."

"Turn around, Sarah."

She did as Jack told her and there he was, standing in the doorway, with a cell phone to his ear. Sarah dropped the handset and ran to him. He dropped the cell phone and didn't wait for her to reach him. They met midway and embraced. Tears filled both their eyes. Natalie and Carol entered the room and were visibly moved by this happy reunion. A volley of nonstop questions flowed from Sarah to the point that Jack finally had to place his hand over her mouth to quiet her.

"This was all your mom's idea. I think it's supposed to be an early birthday gift. I'm glad this happened. I didn't have a clue about what I was going to get you for your birthday and your mom solved one of my life's biggest problems."

"I couldn't have gotten a better gift. How long are you going to be here? Are you staying with us? When did you get here?"

Jack had to cup his hand over her mouth again which brought a laugh from everyone.

"Me and my mom are here until next weekend.

"That's great. Mom, you are the biggest sneak. I can't believe you pulled this off. Thanks so much."

Sarah ran to her mom and gave her one of those great big mom/daughter hugs. She moved to the side of Carol and thanked her for allowing Jack to come and she hugged her. Then Sarah said, "Wait a minute, now I get it. I was wondering why we weren't starting our formal ministry until Wednesday. You mean we have two whole days to ourselves?"

"Happy Birthday, Sarah, you deserve a little break," Natalie said.

Sarah and Jack were inseparable over the next two days. Guided tours had been arranged for the kids and their moms and everything went off as planned. The pulse of the pedestrian and automobile traffic in Tokyo overwhelmed the four sightseers but soon they were accustomed to the hectic pace and fell in step with the masses. The weather cooperated with sunny, clear days and cool evenings. They were exposed to new foods to which they hadn't been accustomed like sushi and Kobe beef, but nothing stopped them from experiencing everything that their senses could absorb. Occasionally, someone recognized Sarah and asked for her healing graces. She was only too happy to comply and brought renewed life, both spiritually and physically, to everyone she encountered.

Friday evening came so quickly for the two young friends. This would be their last time together for quite some time and Sarah promised to stay awake for as long as she could.

During the week, Sarah repeatedly thanked her mom, Jack and Carol Wancsak for giving her the best birthday gift ever. Bearing witness to so much pain and suffering coupled with the long hours attending to the faithful was a daily drain on Sarah's spirit. Having her best friend with her, be it a limited time, meant the world to Sarah. She referred to it as the recharging of her internal batteries. The two young friends relished the weekly calls when Jack was back in the States, but the calls couldn't compare to the personal contact of being together. The schedule for her ministry was set into the next two years so no one could make any commitments as to when the two would see each other again. Perhaps over the summer break from school, Sarah and Jack could visit wherever she was in the world but nothing definite could be arranged at this time.

For their last meal together, they all agreed it best to order in. The quiet surroundings of the hotel suite were greatly preferred. Sarah's notoriety now that her ministry was in full swing caused large crowds to maintain a vigil outside of her hotel. Any attempt to leave would result in an overwhelming onslaught that would limit their private time together. Sitting around the table, they ate very slowly, attempting to make this final few hours together last as-long-as possible. At times, the conversation was awkwardly non-existent. Sensing the uneasiness, Natalie finally spoke.

You know, this wasn't meant to be a wake. You two should be happy for the time you had together this week. I'm not sure when we can do this again but appreciate this time and look forward to the next."

"I know you're right, Mrs. Martinelli," Jack said. "But I think you know by now how much I care for Sarah. For years I had the opportunity to talk to her every day at school and around the neighborhood, but I was dumb and avoided her. Now that she is in my life, our time is rationed out and it's tough to deal with this."

"Jack is right, Mom. He is the only contact I have to my life back home. Don't you think I miss being in school with my friends and teachers? Don't you think I miss jumping in the car with you and driving to the mall and spending our Saturdays together, without the crowds pressing in on all sides? Don't you think I miss my room in our old house; it was like my personal sanctuary. So yes, I'm very sad; I have the right to be. I don't know when I'll see him again. Am I being selfish? I guess I am. Jesus told me I will lead a normal life and have a family. I can't imagine how that will ever happen. Look at my schedule and look at the demands made on me. How can this life be normal for anyone? Help me, Mom, to get through this."

Natalie sat in a semi-state of numbness. All outward appearances indicated that things were going well for her daughter. But all the pent-up emotions finally surfaced for the first time and it totally caught her off guard. She prayed throughout each day for her daughter. She prayed for Sarah's safety. She prayed for peace and stability in her life. She prayed to the Spirit for guidance that she would never falter as a mother and alter the path chosen for Sarah. But now the path was littered with doubt, anxiety and apprehension. Her young Sarah was beginning to stumble and as a mother she must quell these misgivings and smooth the road for her to follow.

"I completely understand what you are going through and wish there was an easier way for you to follow the path set before you, but there isn't. All the blessings you have received have come from God; your very life. In his divine wisdom he chose you for this mission that so far has positively affected thousands if not millions of lives. He has been there to guide your every step and smoothed the way. How can there be any doubts? How can you not be patient and allow your life to proceed as he has intended? Why are you rushing things?

"Your father and I met, and our courtship time created some of my most cherished memories. We didn't rush to the altar but savored every day together. When we knew the time was right we exchanged our vows and started our lives together as husband and wife. Of course, we didn't know the future and the events that would unfold. But we placed our trust in each other because of the strong love that we shared. Our marriage was blessed by God and every day I am thankful for that love.

"I know that someday your father and I will be together again, and I wait in anticipation for that to happen. But in the meantime, I have you to care for and love. It is my main reason for living. You see, this is my mission and I want God to be happy with me. I want to do everything I can for you to be successful, that includes your wellbeing. You have had the better part of a week together. Cherish these memories and look forward to your next vacation together. You are only eleven. I know that sounds rather absurd considering the responsibilities resting on your shoulders. Your life will go on, you will mature to adulthood and have a family of your own. But all in good time. Right now, you need to stay focused on your mission, that is where God wants you. You made the commitment to follow God on this journey and you must follow his lead, step by step. All that has happened and will happen in your life has been preordained. Avoid these temptations of doubt and give in to God's will. Let

God set your path and follow it faithfully and without hesitation. He is counting on you. Mankind is counting on you."

Sarah stared at her mother and sat speechless for some time. She marveled at her insight and sensitivity. Everything she said made sense and soon she felt all her fears and doubts fade and replaced by renewed faith and hope.

"Mom, how did you become so smart?" And with those simple words, she dove into Natalie's outstretched arms. Sarah looked into her mother's eyes and found the peace that was temporarily lacking in her soul. She understood the message from her mother and she felt the strength and conviction returning to her very core.

Carol Wancsak was so overwhelmed with emotion at witnessing this transformation that she burst into tears. Jack went to his mother and consoled her and promised to be patient and allow their lives to unfold as God intended.

The rest of the evening was spent reminiscing about the great times they had experienced during the past week. They accessed the pictures on their cameras and promised to make copies and share them with each other.

Carol and Jack got an early start the next morning. They wanted to avoid any interaction with the crowds and would need all day Sunday to recoup from the long trip and prepare for the coming week. The good-byes and hugs were too numerous to count, so were the tears. But the two young friends knew that this time of separation was unavoidable and that someday, if the relationship was authentic, they would share their lives together forever.

Chapter 10

As a pebble drops into a pond of still water, a ripple emanates outward and continues unimpeded. So it was with the effects of Sarah's mission. Her mission was to be one of compassion for the physically, mentally and spiritually impaired. The healing process was to be the catalyst that would alter people's lives and create positive change; change that would spawn a new era of peace among all peoples no matter their age, gender, religion or heritage. Each person experiencing the healing graces of God sensed this serenity, this calm, this harmony. It was as though each touched the face of God and was transformed into the creation God always intended. This encounter granted each recipient a brief glimpse into the very Spirit of God; His true nature was revealed. And with this vision came enlightenment, one of faith, the belief in God and of His love for humanity. It was acknowledged that God desired for us all to have eternal life with him after our short stay in this physical realm.

With the transformation of each soul, others were likewise positively affected. Parents of children that were healed fell on bended knee and thanked God for their miracle. Their most precious child was saved from a debilitating ailment or even worse, death. They were given a second chance to focus on loving and nurturing their child and dedicating their lives to each other. Children of ailing parents were grateful that the pain and suffering had ceased, and they would have their parents in their lives for a while longer. Friends and neighbors rallied in support of each other, putting aside bitterness and the misunderstandings that always cause conflicts. Where once there was hatred, love prevailed. Where once there was jealousy, understanding prevailed. Where once there was greed, restraint prevailed. People of all nations came to realize there was a true, living God intent on saving his creation from damnation. His outward sign of healing represented that link between God and man that was necessary to awaken the long-lost faith that was cast aside by so many over many millennia.

At first, these changes occurred in small pockets, centered around Sarah's ministry. But soon these small pockets touched and merged and created large areas of peace and tranquility. The faithful in these ***conversion centers*** understood God's commandments of love and lived their lives accordingly, as God ordained.

Sarah's ministry continued for the next ten years. It was a whirlwind tour of the world for our little disciple of the Lord. She continued to fulfill her responsibilities with the focused strength obtained from God. Wherever she traveled, she was welcomed with open arms and open hearts.

During this time, she maintained her relationship with Jack which grew and blossomed. At age twenty-one she married her longtime friend and confidante. They chose their hometown for the wedding respecting their parent's request.

Sarah lamented the fact that Fr. Mark would not be there to celebrate her wedding mass; he had passed away a few years earlier. He was found in his garden, lying among his rows of vegetables, dead from an apparent heart attack. Sarah temporarily suspended her ministry to fly home for his funeral. Over the years she had remained close to Fr. Mark and often sought his guidance. She loved his sense of humor and was quick to exchange little barbs and innuendoes. He would be sorely missed.

The wedding went as planned with Bishop Wallace as the celebrant in his diocesan cathedral. To say it was a crowded affair would be an understatement. Dignitaries from every nation of the world sent letters of intent to attend but most were rejected. Over the ten years of her ministry Sarah had traveled to virtually every corner of the world and touched an incalculable number of souls. This response from world leaders was their way of showing appreciation for her many years of service. But Sarah and Jack wanted as little fanfare as possible and tried to keep the invited guests to a reasonable number. Still, the roadways and sidewalks were jammed with well-wishers, many of whom had experienced the healing graces of God at Sarah's hands.

As they began their married life together, they somehow found more and more time to be together. Jack was rooted in his community because of his landscaping business. He now had a fleet of trucks and over one hundred employees. The notoriety of his association with Sarah over the years did nothing but aid in the growth of his lawn care service and on many occasions, he had to turn new clients away due to the lack of an available workforce.

Sarah and Jack led as normal a life as possible under the circumstances and soon were expecting their first child. The pregnancy went well with few complications, mainly exhaustion from her daily routine. But as the due date drew near, Sarah suspended her ministry and returned home for the delivery. It was late Friday and she and Jack were preparing a nice, quiet evening together. She was curled up in his arms on the sofa when a feeling spread through her entire body. She felt the first contractions and knew the time was near. She called her mother and Jack's mom and alerted them of her status. They both insisted on coming to the house and were there in record time. There was much love in that house that evening as hugs and smiles of reassurance were exchanged. Soon the contractions came more frequently, and Sarah's water broke. It was time to proceed to the hospital and turn to the professionals for the labor and delivery of this precious package.

The labor went well. Sarah wanted the birth to be natural, so no drugs were used. Eight hours later the blessed event occurred. Neither Sarah nor Jack wanted to know the gender of the child during the pregnancy so when they were presented with a healthy boy, they both broke down and cried out of joy and gratitude. A slight tap on the bum and the little fellow let out a wail that surprised even the most seasoned of nurses. After his passageway was cleared and he was wrapped in a receiving blanket, he was placed on Sarah's chest. She brushed his hair into a slight part with her finger and stared into his open eyes. He was a curious little guy who seemed to possess an inquiring look.

Sarah said, "What's going on in that little brain of yours? What are you thinking about?"

A broad smile appeared on his face as though he understood and recognized his mother's voice. Sarah bent down and kissed his forehead and he let out a sigh. She continued to marvel at this new creation of God and to study his features.

Sarah said to Jack, "I guess it's time we should give him a name. I've been thinking of a name for a boy for quite some time now and want to pass it by you."

Jack said, "I'm all ears."

"I would like to name him after the two most important men that have been in my life. I like the name Michael Jack or MJ for short."

"Considering your delicate condition, I wouldn't want to argue with you right now. MJ it is".

Sarah reconnected with her bundle of joy and said, "How does MJ sound to you?" But her voice fell on deaf ears. MJ was at rest after the birthing ordeal and had the most serene, peaceful look on his angelic face. Natalie and Carol were brought into the room and gathered around the bed. They each took turns extolling the beauty of their grandchild and couldn't wait until they could hold the child and marvel at the experience.

Sarah and Jack were blessed with three more children over the next five years. He often would kid her about being a nonstop baby machine and equated her to a rabbit on many occasions.

With each day, Sarah felt her ministry was coming to an end. She sensed this by the ever-decreasing number of faithful coming to her for help. The originally never-ending lines now shrank to manageable numbers each day. On occasion, so few people arrived for the healing that she was done by midday. Many days, there were more curious onlookers than those approaching her for her healing touch.

Jack and their children often traveled with Sarah to destinations around the world. With the decreasing demands due to fewer faithful seeking her help, they had more time to spend together. Jack often said that this made up for all the time they had missed being together prior to their marriage.

Sarah prayed each day for guidance. One evening, while she was alone in her hotel room in Rio de Janeiro, her prayers were answered.

"Hello, Sarah, I hope I didn't startle you." It was Jesus, appearing to Sarah.

"My Lord, it has been some time since we've talked. But as always, it's great to see you again." Sarah walked over to Jesus who was waiting with open arms. They embraced then separated. He invited her to join him on the sofa. They proceeded across the room and sat facing each other.

"Jesus, I'm so happy that you answered my prayers and came to visit with me." She paused then continued. "I'm a little confused about my ministry and which way it's going. It seems there is little need for me anymore. Each day the numbers coming to me are diminishing. Some days the number of faithful is so small that I'm left standing with no one to help by noon and sometimes even earlier. Not wanting to sound bold but can you share anything with me? Is my ministry coming to an end? Have we accomplished everything you wanted?"

"Sarah, you have conducted yourself with the upmost of faithfulness and reverence during the last sixteen years. You have followed all my wishes to the letter and have been instrumental in positively affecting millions of lives. Your actions have achieved my desired goals, that is, to rekindle the long-lost love in mankind for God and their fellow man. Once this love spread there was no stopping it. That love ensured a peaceful world, one where the petty bickering and aggression ceased once and for all. Where peoples of every faith and nationality could live together as God intended without worry or hostility. Where mankind worshipped the one true God and removed the barriers from their lives that prevented them from achieving that level of commitment to their creator. You have helped to open their hearts and minds and spirit to understand these important things and accept them without reservation in their lives. Not everyone was helped by your healing graces; not everyone needed it. But the very action of you being there to help those in need created this rippling effect that touched the lives of so many others. This was a difficult time for you. You sacrificed much for which I will forever be grateful. You answered the call to this ministry and you were faithful throughout. But now it is time for you to go home and enjoy your family and enjoy your life. Your ministry is complete."

Sarah sat there in utter amazement. One minute she felt the burden of the world on her shoulders like she did for the last sixteen years, and the next minute she was free of the responsibility. That burden was removed and with it she felt that weight leave her, and a joy enter her heart that was indescribable. She bent forward and hugged Jesus and whispered into his ear, "Thank you."

"No, it is I who must thank you. I came to you when you were just a little girl and gave you a task that would have been an incredible undertaking for any adult. You accepted my request and were unerring in your fulfillment of your ministry. Now be finally at peace and enjoy your life."

"I have married the man of my dreams as you foretold, and you have blessed Jack and me with four beautiful and healthy children. I don't think I ever really thanked you for all that you have given me in my life. My mother was always there for me and made many sacrifices. These last sixteen years have been tough on her, mainly the worry involved with the lifestyle that we led. But that's all over now. She can enjoy the children as a grandmother should. I'm sure Jack will want to stay in our hometown and that will bring a lot of stability to everyone's lives. He has really been an understanding man in dealing with me. But as he always said, our relationship was something that we both believed in and cherished and nothing was going to keep us apart. We made the best of our limited time together in the past but now we have our whole life ahead of us. You have repeatedly blessed me and for all of these blessing I am eternally grateful".

"You are welcome, Sarah, you are very welcome."

They both embraced and stood up from the sofa. Sarah stared into Jesus' eyes and sensed something was not right, like he wanted to tell her something but was hesitating.

Sarah asked, "What is it, is there something more?"

"I want to brace you for what I am about to tell you. There will soon be a tragedy in your life, one that I cannot stop. This will severely test your faith and that is why I am even telling you."

"What is it, why can't you tell me?"

"Things must unfold accordingly; I must allow things to transpire even if they don't make sense or go against all that is good. You must be strong and be unwavering in your faith. I will be there with you as I always am."

"Dear Jesus, please make this pass. I'm finally to that point where I can lead a normal life and enjoy my family. I've sacrificed everything for you and never asked for anything in return. Can't you grant me this one request?"

"Sweet Sarah, I can't."

"But you are God, you can do anything!"

"Free will has its own implications and that's what complicates this. I don't interfere with people's free will."

"So, you are telling me someone is going to do something bad to me?"

"I can only tell you to be prepared for a tragic event to occur soon in your life. You must be strong and rely on your faith and trust in God to see you through it."

"See me through it! That means that this tragedy will occur to someone in my life, someone that I love. Not one of my children, please, no!"

"I can't tell you anymore. I will just repeat that you must be strong and rely on your faith to get you through the trying time."

"If that is all you can tell me then I accept it. I promise I will keep my faith no matter what impact this has on my life."

"I promise you, I will be there to help you."

"Thank you, Jesus. Thank you once again."

"Sarah, I love you." Sarah moved forward, and they embraced. Jesus wrapped himself around her and hugged her. She found the comfort and safety she so sorely needed. He gently kissed her on the forehead and vanished from her presence.

With his exit, Sarah felt an emptiness suddenly encompass her soul. For the last sixteen years she knew Jesus was with her every minute of every day. But now that her ministry was over, and she no longer possessed the healing graces of God, a deep remorse flowed through her. She thought of all the adventures she had experienced. She thought of all the grateful faces she was privileged to see every day after their healing. She reminisced how she was always the center of attention no matter where she was. Now, she no longer had Jesus in her life, she no longer had the faithful begging for her healing touch, she no longer had the excitement of the world at her feet. She sank into a deep state of depression. She could only equate it to someone completing a very challenging job and then suddenly having a void in their life due to the completion of the job requirements.

Sarah walked over to her bed and knelt to pray for God's guidance. She closed her eyes and lowered her head and prayed for relief of this uncertainty. As she continued with her prayer she felt a warmth flow throughout her entire being. She instantly recognized this as the warmth she had experienced on the many occasions while in the presence of Jesus. She heard a voice that simply said, "Peace be unto you."

She smiled and opened her eyes and a tear trickled down her cheek. There, sitting on her bed, was a single red rose. It emanated such a beautiful bouquet that Sarah though her entire room was full of vases of the most aromatic flowers. But only the one rose was there as a sign from God to help quell her fears and give her peace. She picked up the rose and held it to her chest. She thought, such a simple gift but one that came from God. The gift may have been a simple one but one that came with the relief of all her anxiety. This rose never wilted, never died, and always filled her home with the sweetest of fragrances.

Chapter 11

Quite a few individuals were required in support of Sarah's ministry. Transportation, housing, meals, and site locations were just a few of the areas that were managed for her and all these dedicated people were relieved of their duties. Sarah had gotten to know them on a very personal level and considered them her family away from home. It was difficult for her and them to let go but they had no choice. This chapter in her life was coming to an end and it was necessary to say the sorrowful good-byes.

The arrangements for her journey home were made and confirmed. She boarded the jet with both sorrow in her heart that her ministry was completed but also with great joy that her life with Jack and her children would now commence with no restrictions and no distractions. She had longed for this time and it had finally arrived. She felt like a giddy little girl every time she dared to imagine what it would be like to be that full time mom that she so desperately wanted. But it was now within her grasp and within a few hours she would be home and in the arms of her husband and family.

News of her return hit the media. Many thousand, who had been blessed by her healing touch wanted to welcome her home for the last time and crowded the small airport where she would land. A grandstand was erected for her to address the gathered masses and an area was set aside for all the flowers, stuffed animals, personalized cards and letters that her followers brought to the event in honor of her.

It was a bright sunny afternoon when the wheels of the craft touched the runway. The jet taxied to the hangar where the faithful were gathered. The jet came to a halt and within a few minutes, the exit door was lowered. Sarah was the first to exit which brought the crowd to life. Cheers and applause were raised to a level that rivaled any sports event while a mixture of laughter and tears spread over the faces of the attendees. Sarah was naturally overwhelmed at this outpouring of love and support that she too broke into tears of joy and appreciation. She exited the plane and approached the microphone that was set on the grandstand.

"Thank you, thank you, thank you from the bottom of my heart." The cheers and applause just increased that much more. After many attempts to quiet the crowd, they responded and allowed Sarah to address them.

"Thank you all once again for being here today and thank you for your continued support and prayers over these many years." The crowd erupted again, and Sarah made every attempt to quiet them which after a while was becoming more and more futile.

"I was chosen by God to deliver a message to all mankind. That message was one of faith and hope but mainly of love; the intense love that God has for all his creation. Many people accepted the message they heard while some hardened their hearts and refused to listen and amend their lives. We should continue to pray for those individuals that their hearts and minds are opened to his words. But for we who have heard and believe there is no denying the truth that has been revealed. It is God's desire that we all share eternal life in him. We achieve this everlasting gift by obeying God's commandments of love.

The day will soon come when our Lord and Savior returns to reconcile all things. Will you be prepared to face our Lord in judgment for your actions here on earth? You must be prepared for you know not when he comes. This message I have delivered was just for that purpose; for you to change your lives in a positive way and be prepared for your judgment day. There can be no denying that what we bore witness to is authentic. God exists, and we will all be held accountable for our actions. Be prepared, love one another and love God. This is his message." She paused before saying her final good-bye.

"I would like to thank you once again and for the last time for all of the love you have shown me and for all of the prayers you have offered up for me. I can never thank you individually but know I will continue to pray for you and will forever be grateful for all that you have done for me. I will never know the kind people who paid in full our mortgage or made the monthly utility payments. I will never know the individuals who prepared the never-ending meals for me and my mom, so I could concentrate on my ministry without distraction. I will never know the financiers who underwrote the costs for our transportation and living expenses. I will never know all the countless believers who prayed for my success. God knows who you are and will reward you a hundredfold for your generosity. But now it is time for me to say good-bye. I have a husband and four children that now will occupy my time. I was happy to do what was requested of me but now it is time for me to move on. Once I cared for millions, now I will care for just five. Thank you and God bless you."

With those closing words she waved to her supporters and blew them a kiss. She turned from the microphone and left the stage and into private life.

It didn't take Sarah long to nestle into a lifestyle of a suburban wife and mother. The children demanded so much of her time that she soon put all thoughts of her previous ministry behind and devoted herself to her family. Jack's business was thriving, so they were comfortable when it came to their finances. She occasionally received anonymous offers from a grateful individual she had helped in the past but always declined to accept the gifts no matter how small. Whenever in public, people respected her privacy and were satisfied just to wave and smile. They seemed to sense her need to avoid the public's eye and enjoy being just an ordinary housewife and mother. All was going well for years until that tragic day.

Chapter 12

It was late summer and the thoughts of returning to school were on everyone's mind. Sarah and her family, accompanied by her mom Natalie, decided to spend the day at the mall to load up on school supplies and clothing. The kids were growing as fast as weeds and would need new apparel to replace the flood pants and tight shirts that currently comprised their wardrobe. The time in the mall just flew by and in the late afternoon, they decided to make their way to the food court and feast on the variety of kid pleasing entrees.

As usual, everyone wanted something different, so it took almost a half hour before all the food was purchased and all were seated at the table. Sarah was sitting next to Jack and they each watched while the kids consumed the mall food with such vigor and enthusiasm. At first, they laughed at the sight but soon turned to each other with a look of contentment and satisfaction. These were their children, born out of the love they had for each other. As if on cue, they bent toward each other and kissed and hugged. Seeing this, the kids let out a loud yuck which brought a blush to Sarah's cheeks. Jack jumped up and ran to each of the kids and smothered them in kisses and raspberries, always their favorite. He returned to his seat and joined in the laughter at the table. Life was good.

It was a surreal moment. Out of nowhere, a crazed man with a hunting knife raised high in the air was charging toward their table. He was heading straight toward Sarah. Natalie was the first to see his advances and jumped from her seat. Seeing his intended route toward her daughter, she threw her body in his path to protect Sarah. Wanting to eliminate this obstacle he came down with the knife with incredible force into his victim's chest. The blade split through Natalie's sternum and pierced her heart. Out of love and an overwhelming desire to save her family she clung to the assailant and refused to let go even thought she was severely wounded. Jack jumped from his seat, knocking the chair over in his haste to get to Natalie. A mall guard who was on break and sitting a few tables away leaped to his feet and charged to the scene. Natalie's remarkable efforts allowed Jack and the guard time to get to the perpetrator before he could continue with his intended deed. They wrestled him to the floor and the guard used his handcuffs to secure the man's hands behind his back. He immediately radioed for help and sat on the man until help could arrive.

Sarah ran to her mother and caught her just as she released her grip of the man when he was tackled. She lowered Natalie to the floor and rested her head on her lap. Blood was flowing from the wound. Sarah was afraid to remove the blade thinking the blood would flow even more. She hugged her mom then released the hug and their eyes met.

"Mom, I'm so sorry, this happened because of me. You stopped that man from attacking me, why? I should be lying on the floor and not you."

In a labored breath, Natalie forced her words. With tear filled eyes, she said, "My sweet Sarah, I could never have let that happen. I'm your mother and to my last breath I will always protect you." Natalie had to pause again, her breathing was becoming more labored. "You have made me the most-proud mother by your courage and your love. I have no regrets"

Natalie reached up and touched Sarah gently on the cheek. "I know I'm not going to make it, it's my time. I love you my little angel"

"No, Mom, please hold on. Help is on the way. Please don't give up!"

A gush of tears flowed from Sarah's redden eyes and streamed down her cheeks. As they dripped from her chin, they merged with Natalie's and began to pool. As Sarah was staring into her mother's eyes, she perceived a faint light reflecting from the pool of tears. Sarah looked up to see a soft, muted light emanated from above that rested on and bathed her mother's face. Everyone standing around gasped in disbelief of this vision. Looking into the light, Natalie uttered her last word, "Michael." The soft light faded, and her body went limp in Sarah's arms; she knew instantly that her mother had passed.

"No, no, no, Mommy, no. This can't be. Why, why did this have to happen? Why didn't you stop it? Why didn't you take me instead?" She was on the verge of cursing our Lord when she stopped herself and remembered her last encounter with Jesus. He had foretold of a tragic event that was eminent in her life. She remembered that the gift of free will affected most of the decisions in life and that this man had chosen to do a horrific deed and it was not God's fault.

With clarity of thought, she put those angry feelings aside and concentrated on the remaining time with her mother. She realized that this would be the last time she would ever spend with her and that soon all that would remain would be the memories. She continued to hold her mother until the authorities arrived on the scene.

Sarah and her family lived through the pain of the funeral.The numbers attending the viewing and service were incalculable. The outpouring of love for Sarah and her family concerning their loss helped to ease the pain. But Sarah knew she could never fill the void created by her mother's death.

The days following Natalie's funeral, Sarah understandably fell into a deep state of depression. She couldn't reconcile what had happened and needed help. A week had gone by and Jack sensed the changes in Sarah and knew he had to do something to alleviate her pain. After Jack got the kids to bed, he entered their bedroom where he found Sarah lying in bed curled in the fetal position, sobbing into a tissue. He came to the bed and sat next to her.

"Sweetheart, I can see how this has affected you. That man took away from you a person who not only was your mother but probably your best friend. There is no rationale behind why this should have happened so for all these reasons I can understand why you feel the way you do. But I can't stand by and let this eat away at you. Your children need you, I need you. Do you want to talk about it?"

Sarah wiped the tears from her eyes and face. She sat up in bed and leaned forward and let Jack hold her in his comforting arms. She always found refuge in her Jack and needed him now more than ever. She burrowed down deep into his embrace attempting to find a sanctuary of peace and love, the one thing that she thought she had obtained after her ministry but was wiped away by one vicious act. After a while, she relaxed enough that Jack raised her into a sitting position in front of him. He cupped her face and with his thumbs, whisked away the remaining tears. She smiled out of appreciation of his gentleness.

"Over the past week, I've had time to think about my parents and how their lives seemed like riding on a rollercoaster. They had the high of romancing each other, dating, getting married and sharing a few years together as husband and wife. Then there came the low after my dad was killed. Then there was the high of having a healthy child and the joys that come with parenthood. Next came the low due to the constant worry for the safety of her child while she was conducting an extraordinary mission for God. Then came the high in gratitude that the ministry was over, and her child was safe and had found the man of her dreams and was starting to raise a family of her own. Do you see what I mean? My parents were remarkable people to have gone through all of these changes and never actually have any consistency in their lives together."

Jack sat there speechless, not knowing how to respond.

"I know this is difficult for you to grasp," Sarah said. "Unless you've been there and witnessed it, it can be unsettling. Look at your family; a mom and dad who have been there for each other and raised three healthy children. Now they are blessed with eight grandchildren who love them. Both of your parents are still young and have many years left to enjoy each other and these kids and grandkids."

Jack continued to remain silent.

"What's really amazing is how both of my parents died. Both sacrificed themselves for another person and both were wounded in the heart. But what's even more amazing are their last words. I don't know if I ever told you the story but when my dad died, his last words were, 'tell my wife that I love her'. He whispered this with his dying breath to the corpsman that was at his side. And when my mother was lying in my arms, there was the light that glowed on her face and what was her last word, 'Michael'. You were there and witnessed that. But do you see the similarities in their deaths? There was an intertwining of their lives that transcended even into death. They lost their lives coming to the aid of another and had each other as the focal point as they drew their last breath. They were such unique people that loved life and had an immeasurable love for each other. But it's all gone now, and I feel so empty. I know I have you and the kids and a wonderful life, but I've been cheated, they've been cheated.

"Jesus and I talked many times about free will and its virtues and shortcomings. When used in the right manner, it can make a positive and remarkable difference in so many lives. But when used in a destructive way, can adversely affect and devastate many lives. Using free will and making the decision to commit a horrific deed, that man, in one savage act, killed my mom. His actions caused a rippling effect of so many negative emotions in me. I sensed fear, sorrow, anger, hatred and the need for revenge; I wanted that man to suffer like I was suffering. But I know that's not right. I need to make peace with God over this. He forewarned me of an impending tragedy, but I didn't want to accept it. I blocked it out until it was too late, and then it happened. Now I'm left with all this sadness and emptiness that is eating me alive. It's time for me to pray to God for help so I can get out of this slump and get back to living. I know the first thing I need to do is forgive that man, but I don't know if I can. I'm going to need the healing graces of the Spirit to reconcile and end these feelings. I know I'll always miss my mom, but I have the wonderful memories of her in my life and I'll have to cling to them. That's all I've got now."

Jack was amazed at the turnaround in Sarah's attitude. Within the period of one short hour, she had reasoned through all the turmoil and misgivings and come to a peaceful conclusion in her life.

"You are remarkable," he said. "I don't know of another person who could have gone through what you have and still come out of it with their sanity intact. Your faith is so strong that I envy you. I know now that you'll be okay."

They embraced and for the first time since the funeral, Sarah had a restful night's sleep.

For her own peace of mind and seeking some type of closure, Sarah had to know why the killer wanted to attack her. The trial hadn't begun and there was word that a plea of insanity might be forthcoming. She contacted the District Attorney's office and received permission to visit with the accused.

When the date for the visit arrived, Sarah went to the county jail accompanied by Jack. They agreed that Sarah alone would meet with the defendant. Jack kissed her and told her to be strong as she left his comforting touch.

Sarah was led through a maze of secure corridors, with barred doors being unlocked before them and locked after them. She was finally brought to a small meeting room usually reserved for the defendants to meet with their legal counsel. When she entered the room, he was already seated at the small table that was centered in the room. His hands were shackled to his feet by long chains that rattled every time he moved. The repeated sound of the chains rattling made Sarah uncomfortable. She sat opposite from him in the only other chair in the room. Two guards remained in the room, one behind him and one at the door. At first, she felt ill at ease; his stare seemed to drill right through her. But soon, her confidence was restored. She raised her eyes and looked into the eyes of the man who had killed her mother.

"What do you want with me?" he said. "Why did you come here, to gloat? I'm not sorry for what I did, so don't look for an 'I'm sorry' from me. You should be the one cold and rotting in the grave. If I could have pushed that woman aside I could have gotten to you. But she hung on; I never knew a woman could be so strong. I didn't get to you, but you lost your mother, so I guess I'll have to be satisfied with your suffering and pain."

"How does a person get to this level of anger and hatred? What happened to you that you felt it imperative to attack me in front of my children? You obviously know who I am and what I've accomplished with my life. Tell me, I need to know."

The man leaped from his seat but was restrained by his shackles. The guard standing behind the man pushed him back in the chair. Removing his baton from his belt, the guard hit the man across the back with a heavy blow. The man screamed out in pain and went into a tirade of profanity against his assailant then turned his anger toward Sarah. The guard hit him again, attempting to quiet him.

"Stop hitting him," Sarah screamed. "Let him alone."

This shocked the guard who was only trying to protect Sarah from the man's attack.

The man settled in his chair and looked at Sarah.

"Why do you care what he does to me? I killed your mother, you should hate me. What's your angle here? I asked you before, what do you want from me?"

"I need to know why you came after me and my family. Is that so difficult to understand?"

"Why should I care what you want? As I see it, I'm the one in the driver's seat."

"So that's it, you don't want to tell me?"

"If I do, what's in it for me? You know how it works, you give a little and you take a little."

"I have nothing more to give. You took from me one of the most important people in my life. What else do I have to give?"

The man remained quiet. You could see the gears spinning full force in his mind behind those evil eyes. How was he going to get over on Sarah? How was he going to make her suffer even more? By telling her the reason behind his irrational actions he believed he could open the wounds of her sorrow even wider and land the fatal emotional blow.

"All right, I'll come clean. You want to know, I'm going to tell you. Do you know who I am, do you know my name?"

"Yes, you are Frank Wetzel. I don't know you and I've never met you before that awful day. Why?"

"It's all about the last name that should give you a hint. When we were growing up, my younger brother got a nickname. Wetzel morphed into Weasel. Johnny Wetzel, The Weasel, was my brother. Does that help?"

Sarah sat there and had to think for a minute, and it finally hit her. Early in her ministry, the man named Rocco came to her with his mother in the hopes of healing her Alzheimer's disease. She had the unexpected encounter with Rocco that immediately came to mind. When she held Rocco's hand and his miserable life of crime came flashing before him, she was witness to all the violence and darkness in that life. And it was Weasel that was his last victim before he came to her for his mother's healing.

"This has to do with Rocco, doesn't it?"

"Bingo, babe, you got it. You're pretty smart."

"But I still don't understand. Rocco killed your brother. What does that have to do with me?"

"After he met you, Rocco somehow changed. He left all his dirty dealings behind and became legit. This took him off the streets. I couldn't get to him. I knew he was the one that killed Johnny, but I couldn't get to him. He was constantly surrounded by business people in places that weren't accessible to me. When he drove, he always used a chauffeur who was armed for his security. For the most part, he stayed pent up in that mansion of his which had around the clock security. I'm not a high-tech kind of guy and couldn't get past his alarms and cameras. So, there you have it, Rocco killed my brother and I couldn't get to him. I couldn't have my revenge. By your actions and doing whatever you did to him, you took away my getting revenge against him. I had to settle the score one way or the other. I couldn't let him get away with Johnny's murder. So, if I couldn't get to him, I knew eventually I could get to you. I waited; boy, did I have to wait. But I knew that at some time you would come back to our town, I just had to be patient. It took almost twenty years, but I got my revenge. It wasn't against Rocco, so I had to settle for the second-best thing. And you know, in a way I think it's better that I got to your mom. Now you're still alive and have the pain of that loss in your life, just like the pain I feel every day.

"I now have only one regret, I didn't take out more of your family. I wanted to get to you with a knife. You see, knives are much more personal than guns. With a knife, you get to see the horror in your victim's eyes as you sink the blade into their body. You miss all of that with a gun. But with a gun I could have popped you, your old man, your kids, your mom and anyone else who would try to stop me. Oh well, I guess you just can't have everything."

Frank Wetzel sat there with a smirk on his face knowing he had delivered the fatal emotional blow that he desired. And the wounds were opened wider for Sarah and the emotions started to flow, tears welled in her eyes. This whole thing made no sense to her at all. She was following God's will and serving the faithful when Rocco came into her life. The visions or whatever they were had nothing to do with her ministry, but she was subjected to the encounter and did what she had to get through it. When Rocco reformed his life, she was happy for him and that she had a part in his conversion. But now, twenty years later, her former actions caused the death of her mother; someone totally innocent and removed from the matter. Why, she thought? She burst into tears for her loss, but more so for her mother whose life was prematurely ended by a vengeful man.

Overcome by the wide spectrum of emotions she sat there in a state of numbness, not knowing what to do next. He had won. He had driven home the final blow that summed up his hatred for her and the sweetness of his revenge. How was she to leave this place? He had control over her. She felt his hatred pushing her deeper into her chair. She felt she couldn't get up even if she wanted to. Oh please, Lord, help me. She kept repeating these words over and over in her mind. After what seemed an eternity, her prayers were answered. Deep inside her mind, deep within her heart, deep within her soul she heard his comforting voice; the voice she longed for, the voice she hadn't heard for many years. The words were simple in nature but packed with a powerful message, "Peace be unto you."

Immediately, Sarah's heart was healed. She felt all the sorrow leave which was replaced by a sense of calming and relief; the relief that comes when you trust in the Lord and put all things in his hands. She thought of a sermon that Fr. Mark gave one Sunday. He had said that we should bring all our worries and troubles to the Lord and place them on the altar. We should offer these problems in our life, some small and some large to God. By doing so, we remove the stress from our lives and place our trust and hope in God. Why she remembered that sermon at this time made no sense to her, but it was like Fr. Mark was reaching from heaven and helping her through this tough time. Her head and heart were finally cleared of all the distractions and she obtained the peace she sought. A faint smile spread across her lips. She removed a tissue from her purse and dried her tears. She pushed her chair back from the table and stood up. She reached down and touched Frank Wetzel on the hand and said three little words, "I forgive you."

With that, she turned and exited the room after the guard at the door let her pass. Wetzel tried everything in his power to chase after her. He jumped up and tried to make his way to the doorway after her. He let out such screams and profanity that he was heard by Sarah well down the maze of hallways. It took the combined efforts of both guards to restrain him. His loud, abusive screams brought two other attending guards to the room and all four got him back to his cell.

The entire encounter with his intended victim had backfired. He wanted her to leave as a crushed woman, one so overcome with emotions that she would sink to the lowest of lows and never get up. He needed that final revenge for the loss of his brother; he needed her to continue to suffer.

He continued to scream and yell from his cell. The hatred emanated from his very core. In the end, she had won, and he had lost.

Sarah met Jack in the waiting area where they embraced. He was naturally curious, and she promised that she would fill him in on all the details when they got home. Right now, she was happy to be with her Jack and nothing else mattered.

Chapter 13

Their children grew and one by one went away to college. They found their soul mates and married and had children. Their children matured and had their own children. All the while, Sarah and Jack were the anchors of peace and security in their lives. One time, a friend of Sarah's asked how she got along with her kids and their kids and their kids. Sarah simply answered, "They still come home."

So, it came to pass, that Sarah aged with grace and the love of her man at her side. But as with all things in life, the end inevitably came. Well into her nineties, Sarah had a disabling fall that seemed to start the decline of her health. Almost every day, Jack would tell her to pray to God for a healing of her own, but she resisted. She would always say that that part of her life was over, and she must now prepare to see God for the last time; a time that would last for all of eternity.

It was a Sunday afternoon when it happened. She was at home in her bed just like she requested. Jack and all the generations surrounded the bed. To say the room was crowded would be an understatement; they all loved this blessed woman. The only dry eye in the house was Sarah's. She knew soon she would be in the presence of God and nothing could distract her from that end. She looked around the room at all her loved ones and a sense of uncontrollable joy and happiness filled her heart.

A flood of memories rushed through her mind. She thought about her relationship with her Jack and the difficulties they'd had in their early relationship but how she had spent a lifetime with the man that she truly loved and knew she was loved in return. The beautiful faces of her children were there before her along with their offspring and the next generation. How can anything compare to the joys of parenthood? And with that, she thought about her mother. She grew up in a home with a parent that was totally dedicated to her, one who never failed her and was always there to guide her through every conceivable situation, and there were quite a few. Then she thought about her dad, the man she never knew but still played an important part in her life. She dwelled on her friends that had been there for her throughout the years and all the support staff that assisted her in her ministry, many of whom kept in contact with her for many years. She thought, what a wonderful life I have led.

She looked around the room one last time, at her Jack and all her offspring. She smiled and uttered her final words, "I love you." With those words she left this earth. Jack felt the grasp she had on his hand eased up as her head lowered against her chest. He reached up and closed the eyes of his wife.

Sarah was laid to rest on a hilltop next to her mother and father. Now in death, they were together.

The news of her passing spread around the world. People of all nations mounted a drive for the immediate canonization of Sarah and her mother to sainthood. There was such an outpouring to the church in Rome by the religious and the laity that their request couldn't be denied. All the prerequisites such as the investigation, the required miracles and approval by the Congregation for the Causes of Saints were bypassed and the Holy Father canonized Sarah and Natalie saints within three months of her death. Now, their names were always mentioned in the same breath, Saints Sarah and Natalie.

Sarah perceived she was leaving her earthly body. There was nothing physical about the event, but she felt she still had her senses. Not the physical senses that we all share but ones that are employed in heaven. You have no body, you are now a spirit like God. But there are senses that are used to communicate with one another and with God and fully take in the beauty and tranquility of your surroundings. She soon realized that there were no words to describe these senses, so she was happy just to call them senses.

Jesus was the first to greet her. She saw him like she had never seen him before, standing there in all his magnificence and glory. It is God's desire for all to obtain the reward of heaven and with it the ability to be in his presence. Sarah stood before Jesus and saw deep into his very soul. His true nature was revealed, and she finally understood all the deep theological mysteries that had plagued mankind for all its existence. God was truly benevolent and loving. She knew now that he so loved his creation and wanted all of us to share in that divine nature with him. She was pulled into his very being and was enveloped by God. His love spread throughout her soul and she became one with her creator. For all of eternity, she would be one with God and his presence would forever be with her.

Natalie and Michael were next to join her with God. It wasn't as though they approached from outside of her circle of consciousness but were already there, they just manifested from within. The love and joy were so intense that Sarah couldn't perceive any description of this encounter. All her life on earth she dreamed of the day when she would be with her mother and father and now that time had arrived. As with God, she would perceive the presence of her loved ones with her throughout eternity in heaven.

Sarah now expanded her consciousness to other parts of her realm. She was overwhelmed at experiencing the contact with the innumerable number of souls already present. Along with each contact came an understanding of the life the individual had led on earth. Upon entering heaven, your entire life on earth becomes like an open book for all to see. Sarah noticed that some led exemplary lives and obeyed God's commandments of love. These souls made the transition into heaven rather easily. Others were not so perfect but before death reconciled with God and justified their existence in heaven. They had to be purified and tempered before obtaining their eternal reward.

The souls that were subjected to eternal damnation were also revealed to Sarah. After some time at contemplating her surroundings, she was more surprised at those who didn't achieve their eternal reward versus those that did.

Over time, earthly time, Sarah welcomed family and friends just as she had been welcomed by her parents. But the most anticipated for her was, naturally, Jack. The love they shared on earth couldn't compare to the love they now possessed. The love on earth was mainly physical. You love the person because they look appealing to you, they are kind to you, they do little things that make you feel good about yourself, and they are there when you need them the most. On occasion, they share of themselves through the act of love and they never betray you or are dishonest with you. But in heaven, their very soul is exposed, and that love is intensified beyond measure. You see the individual for whom they are. Unlike on earth, there is no more hardship and pain, no more misunderstandings, only love in its most pure of states. And that love is ever present because that person is ever present.